Seasons under my Sky

A Collection of Rural Writings

BY

Christopher Hilsdon

Dedication

In memory of my late father, Andrew Hilsdon, who taught me by
example how to recognise and care for the important things.

Proceeds from the sale of this book will be donated to:
The Restoration Fund of St Giles Church, Water Stratford, Bucks.

Introduction

Villagers living in this rural area to the west of Buckingham, in the very middle of England, look forward each month to reading the latest account of farming and country life; I am delighted to introduce these articles to a wider audience. New even to most local readers are the poems, which treat similar countryside themes in a variety of forms and moods, and are crafted with the same care with which the writer ploughs a field or works wrought iron.

Chris Hilsdon has lived and farmed in these parts all his life, as have his family for four generations – a reassuring sense of continuity pervades his thinking. Here you will read memories of farm life half a century ago, as well as learn something of the technology and methods of modern farming. We delight in recognising afresh, through his descriptions, signs of the ever-changing seasons, while also sharing his privileged access to sights, sounds and scents that most of us don't have the opportunity – or the knowledge – to notice. With the eye of an artist, he depicts the 'tapestry' wings of a butterfly and the 'corduroy' appearance of a newly drilled field; with the mind of a scientist, he records the quarter of a million tonnes of water that fell on the farm in ten days of rain and notes which colours of lichen favour particular trees. From his detailed observation of the behaviour of different kinds of birds, insects and other creatures, to his sense of awe when viewing the light of extinct stars, the writer conveys deep appreciation of the world he knows so well.

Chris works with respect for nature, cutting back ivy to protect a tree in such a way as to minimise damage to insects; but without sentimentality, making the case for culling grey squirrels, and recording – with frustration and sometimes wry humour – difficulties posed by weather and bureaucracy. With a sense of history, he sees the profusion of wildflowers which indicates the probable site of a former rick yard, and evokes medieval drovers bringing cattle along these roads on the way to market in London. But most important, perhaps, is the insight we gain into the work of a farmer today, when most of us know shockingly little about how our food, that basic requirement of life, is produced, and rarely stop to think how farming moulds our English landscape.

Churches, like farms, continue to play an important part in country life; this farmer, like his mother, father and grandfather, has been churchwarden of St Giles, Water Stratford, 'the jewel in the crown of the North Bucks churches' according to a former Bishop of Buckingham, and the inspiration for the poem 'My Church'. This little building, beautiful in its simplicity, dates from the 13th Century and is known for fine medieval tympana above the north and south doors. A recently installed stone tablet on the tower wall commemorates its famous 17th Century Rector, Reverend John Mason, proclaimer of the Second Coming of Christ and writer of some of the first English hymns including 'How shall I sing that majesty'. Set in a tranquil churchyard overlooking a pasture field, the church offers peace and inspiration to a regular congregation, as well as to many occasional visitors.

In 2007 we launched an appeal in order to re-roof and repair this much loved church. Our small community has supported this with a will and we have been generously helped by friends from further afield. Thank you for buying this book, and thus contributing to the restoration, so that we and future generations may continue to use and enjoy a place steeped in centuries of prayer and praise. We hope you will see your surroundings afresh through these pages, or may one day visit the area which nurtures the author of these writings.

Sara Edwards

Contents

Spring

Summer

Spring

Yews and Ewes

Timber from conifers is usually classed as softwood, but the wood from a yew tree is tougher and of greater density than most hardwoods. I was reminded of this last month whilst cutting back some boughs from a yew in the churchyard; the tree grows close to the church and its wayward branches had been interfering with the guttering. Unlike many churchyard yews, this is not an ancient specimen, only perhaps two or three hundred years old, but some yews date back many centuries and are often as old as the church itself. There was a time in history when yew trees were planted in almost every parish in order to provide timber for the longbow, once England's most important armament. Blackbirds and thrushes relish the berries, but the evergreen foliage is poisonous to livestock. I suppose that a well fenced churchyard, therefore, was an obvious choice when searching for safe places to plant yews in ages past.

Little grows under the dark canopy of an old yew, but not far away the first violets of spring have appeared, white and purple blooming together in the lee of a hedge, at the base of a large sycamore. The white ones have no scent but the purple ones have one of the first wild fragrances of the year, delicately nostalgic, at once taking you back through the springs of a lifetime. Looking up a few feet above the violets, you see that the hedge is still apparently lifeless; the only colour is provided by lichens growing on twigs and branches and appearing as patches on the trunks of hedgerow trees. Take a closer look and you will find that these strange organisms, which are actually a partnership between fungi and algae, look like miniature clusters of seaweed. Lichens tend to live on older wood; those on ash and elder often have the colour of ochre, whilst the silvery blue and greyish green types seem to prefer field maple, crab and blackthorn. Whatever else may be happening to the climate, the increased prevalence of lichens indicates that the air, at least in this part of England, is cleaner now than it has been for a very long time. As a result, we have found it necessary for the last thirty years or more to apply sulphur to our crops in spring; previously this element was plentifully supplied via an atmosphere which was once polluted by industrial processes.

Free fertilizer from the air may be a thing of the past, but a flock of sheep grazing a pasture leaves behind a wealth of fertility, especially if the sheep are also receiving supplementary feed in troughs. When the hard winter weather arrived, we started feeding our ewes on whole oats: just a small quantity in the troughs to begin with, because sheep take a week or so to get used to a different food. Near to the meadow where they graze is a small lake, created alongside the river about seven years ago. It has naturalised well, and is now the haunt of about twenty Canada geese. I was surprised at how quickly the ewes took to the oats – right from the start the troughs were always completely empty by my next visit. After two days I realised why – the geese had been stopping off to clear up the left-overs, after the sheep had turned away. Dawn breaks a little earlier each day now, and the wild geese can sometimes be seen flying across the pale early morning sky. In towns and cities early signs of spring can pass almost unnoticed, lost in the rush of urban life, where many spend their lives cooped up in buildings or boxed in inside their cars, endlessly battling with traffic. City dwellers will be aware of the milder weather, the subtle changes in the quality of the light and the gradual lengthening of the days, but they have scarce opportunity to appreciate the changing landscape day by day, or to witness at first hand the slowly unfolding mysteries of field and farm, river and wood, as nature reflects the advancing season.

March 2010

Field Names

In these tough times for agriculture, it is all too easy for us farmers to overlook the pleasures and privileges of living and working so close to the land. My house is surrounded by my fields; I don't have to drive to work, it waits for me outside the door. On the other hand, it is sometimes hard to get away from it, but one accepts that farming is not so much a job as a way of life. Working in the fields now that spring is here gives me that sense of being at one with the landscape again. Our activities as farmers today add another layer to the wealth of history created by the generations that have lived off the land before us; it is as though their spirits are still present, shaping the lives of today's farmers and farm workers. The land is very much a place of identity, and each field has its own name, and its own story to tell.

Field names are fascinating as they give clues about former use, ownership or local features, some of which may now be extinct. In the past, names written down were often miss-spelt, and those transmitted by word of mouth (not everyone could read or write) were subject to corruption caused by lazy speech or mispronunciation. This explains why many have changed over time. Some names date from the Saxon period, but others are more recent, originating from the time of The Enclosures, when new fields were created by sub-division. Old tithe maps are a good source of information: they usually show fields with names that were in common use in the 1800s. The current passion for bureaucracy, so beloved by Defra, poses a threat to traditional field names. Farmers are now obliged to identify all their fields by an OS map reference followed by a National Grid field number. Thus one of my fields, known for generations as The Stonepit, (it once contained a quarry) now becomes SP 6434 NG 9077. Common names, such as Dairy Ground, Home Close, Millways, Pond Field and so on, can be found on lots of farms; their origins are self-explanatory. More interesting are names like Brickell Close – a corruption of Brick Kiln Close, though no kiln exists today. Names containing 'holm' are very old, originating from the Norse word 'holmr', meaning land near water. 'Slad' or 'slav' means shallow valley, and 'glebe' is land of the church or parish. 'Knoll' refers to a rise or small hill, and 'mere' suggests moor or mud.

I have a field known as Bittersweet, with easy-working loamy soil at one end, progressively changing to difficult heavy clay at the other. I'm not sure if the name reflects the different soil types, or whether it makes reference to the notoriously variable yield that this field produces from one year to the next. Another field of mine is called Severn Wells, a charming name, but probably the result of Chinese whispers as we are nowhere near the famous river and I'm not aware of any wells in the vicinity. On a neighbouring farm there is a pasture field on a steep bank known as The Rifle Butts, so named because a local division of The Bucks Yeomanry, to which my grandfather and his brothers belonged, practised marksmanship there in the Great War. Mount Pleasant is a field which lies on a hill, rising from the banks of the river to the south of Water Stratford. From here there is a commanding view of St Giles Church and the village. It is generally believed that this field was named by the followers of John Mason, famous rector and hymn writer of Water Stratford in the late 1600s. This is where many of them camped and remained for several years after his death; eventually they became a nuisance and had to be evicted. It is important that traditional field names are preserved; the danger is that once older generations have gone, they could be lost forever.

March 2006

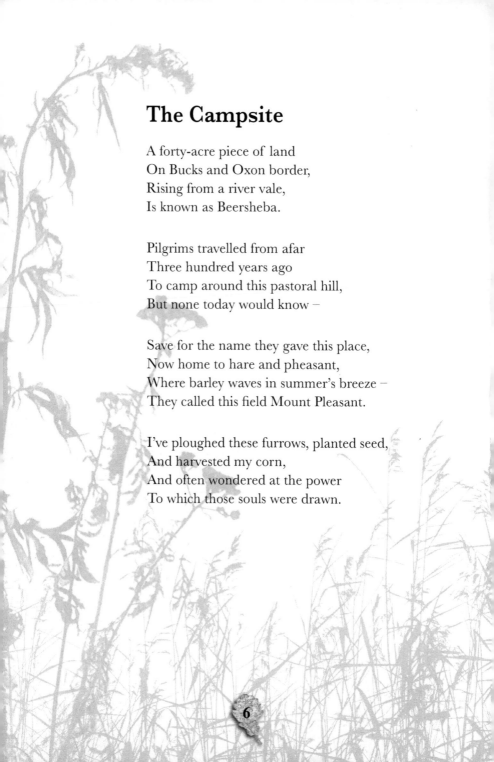

The Campsite

A forty-acre piece of land
On Bucks and Oxon border,
Rising from a river vale,
Is known as Beersheba.

Pilgrims travelled from afar
Three hundred years ago
To camp around this pastoral hill,
But none today would know –

Save for the name they gave this place,
Now home to hare and pheasant,
Where barley waves in summer's breeze –
They called this field Mount Pleasant.

I've ploughed these furrows, planted seed,
And harvested my corn,
And often wondered at the power
To which those souls were drawn.

I've climbed the hill to see below
The village clear in view,
Well known to them as Sion,
Their holy rendezvous.

They came to hear John Mason preach,
Their Christian faith to nourish,
They sang the hymns he'd written here
In Water Stratford parish.

St Giles stands like a rock today,
The church his followers knew,
Where charismatic passion ruled
In pulpit, street and pew.

No idle whim their presence here,
No fad nor strange caprice;
But t'was ordained from heaven above:
May their spirits rest in peace.

The Drainage Charge

Early signs of spring have arrived, and the land is waking from the dead of winter. Birds still visit garden feeders on the harsher days, but the sight of a song thrush flying past with a wisp of dead grass in its beak does much to lift one's spirits. Trees and hedges were still bare in mid-February as one would expect, but during that lovely spell of early spring weather you could see where the new buds would break from. A young weeping willow and a quince, both in sheltered places in the garden, were actually coming into leaf. Sunny days make such a difference – we all crave warmth and light after the dull, dark months. Grass is starting to grow again, but our river meadows remain strewn with flotsam and jetsam, and a couple of fences have been ruined by the pressure of water carrying floating debris which became caught up against them. This is a legacy of the flooding which occurred frequently over the last few months, and which was quite rare years ago. The situation has not been helped by the neglect of our rivers for at least the past two decades.

In the past, responsibility for their maintenance was undertaken by hundreds of local Catchment Boards and River Authorities, the emphasis being on land drainage and flood defence, rather than conservation. A General Drainage Charge was levied on farmers and others occupying land within certain catchment areas of the river, and this money was used to fund the cost of the work. The river was regularly inspected, and problems such as the build-up of silt on bends or fallen trees impeding the flow of water would be dealt with. Every few years the river was dredged, and bank-side willows were managed by pollarding. In 1989, these local bodies were swallowed up into one huge organisation known as the National Rivers Authority. About this time, all maintenance work to the river stopped. In 1996, the NRA itself was abolished, and its responsibilities were taken over by a new and even bigger government creation, the Environment Agency. The General Drainage Charge is, of course, still collected, and last year, 2006, raised over £3 million in the Anglian Region alone. I personally now have to pay £400 per year, for which the stretch of river running through our farm receives absolutely no attention whatsoever. What is needed is a return to regular maintenance programmes, designed to keep the water flowing to minimise flooding, but sensitively managed to take account of conservation.

Last year the EA imposed new rules on farmers concerning the disposal of agricultural waste, one of which instructs on how to deal with ditching spoil. Traditionally, the mud from the bottom of the ditch was always spread on the adjacent land. This is no longer allowed: it must now be deposited only on top of the ditch bank. However, in another set of rules laid down by Defra, it is a punishable offence to place ditching spoil (which they now class as 'waste') anywhere within two metres of the ditch! This is just one example of how increasing regulation results in confusion. You can be sure that the people who dreamed up this nonsense have never cleaned a ditch in their lives.

The wetter, warmer winters of the last few years have sometimes brought spring on a little too soon; a hard frost or two in early March to hold things back a little does no harm. One of the treats of spring are the early flowers; we have already enjoyed aconites, snowdrops, primroses and violets, as much at home in churchyards and gardens as they are in the wild in this season of purity and innocence, which gradually unfolds in its timeless way, transcending all the petty irritations caused by cumbersome and bureaucratic "here today, gone tomorrow" government agencies and departments.

February 2008

Timing and Chiming

How do we know when spring has arrived? According to astronomy the arrival of spring occurs at the time of the vernal equinox, about March 21st. Some would say that spring has come when the ground is dry enough for planting, or when the first buds appear. For others it is when the early daffodils flower, or new-born lambs are seen in the fields. Many of us know that spring is here when we re-discover the resurgence of life in the natural world after the dull torpor of winter, but timing is in any case tricky, and often quite personal.

On the farm, the 'to do' list grows alarmingly, and spreading fertiliser on winter-sown crops has been a priority. The words of the plant science lecturer from my student days come to mind: 'the right amount of the right type in the right place at the right time'. Getting these four elements right is challenging, given all the variables we have to work with. Timing is perhaps the most difficult to achieve, governed as it is by the weather and the prevailing ground conditions. The old agricultural maxim 'There's no fertiliser like the Master's Foot' is as true today as ever. I have been away for a while, and on my return I took a walk round the farm to check up on things in general. I discovered two blocked land drains, some serious damage to my oilseed rape caused by wood pigeons, an excellent frost mould on the fields earmarked for spring planting, and evidence of occupancy of my artificial otter holt. I was quite excited about this for a moment, until I realised that the visitor was not an otter after all, but an inquisitive badger.

The farm is in the Countryside Stewardship Scheme, membership of which generally involves farming in an environmentally sensitive way. The aim is, in a nutshell, to protect and enhance the natural diversity of the countryside. One of our own objectives is to improve and extend wildlife habitats adjacent to the river, which runs along the southern boundary of the farm. Otters were once present here, but in common with the rest of the country, numbers declined steadily from the 1930s for several reasons, not least the pollution of rivers and canals, their main habitat and food source. At one time they were also hunted; I remember a meet of otter hounds at Water Stratford when I was a child, but this practice ended in the 1950s. Water quality is now steadily improving, and otter populations are slowly recovering, but monitoring these shy, nocturnal creatures is difficult.

Otter sightings often turn out to be those of mink – the two are easily confused, even though mink are much smaller and usually darker than otters. The American mink, which originally escaped from fur farms, has unfortunately become naturalised in the UK, and has almost destroyed our native water vole population. Otters have recently been identified on the Ouse near Newport Pagnell; hopefully this means that they might eventually move further upstream. I built my artificial holt from willow logs and brushwood, on the riverbank, two years ago in the hope of encouraging any passing otters. It would be wonderful to see them on our stretch of the river again one day.

On Wednesday March 3rd the cold wintry weather of the past few weeks was gradually being replaced by milder conditions as the day progressed. In the evening we were treated to the enchanting chimes of Shalstone church bells being expertly rung for the first time for many years, following an extensive refurbishment project. As the bells pealed out into the night a gentle warm rain began to fall; it was as though winter had just slipped silently away. For me, spring arrived at that very moment.

March 2004

Lent, and a Bit of Fun

The birds started singing again in mid February, on a day when a few patches of snow could still be seen under north facing banks and hedges. Ten days later, Ash Wednesday marked the beginning of Lent. Easter, although a moveable festival, usually comes about half way through the English spring, with the forty days of Lent being the austere half. Trees remain bare and plants are vulnerable, animals and birds are often frail, weakened by hunger and the struggle to survive the harsh winter months. For many female creatures, the demands of giving birth at this time of year are an additional burden. Spring is characterised by the flowering of some of our oldest native trees, the thorns, which are symbolic in Christian tradition. Depending on the date of Easter, the blackthorn sometimes flowers during Lent. Snowy little blooms emerge in cold weather, from thickets of sharp, forbidding and leafless thorns in a kind of harsh severity, which somehow empathises with both the sorrow and the joy of the Easter message. By contrast, the hawthorn flowers later, when its new leaves are already shining in the warmth of the sun. The soft profusion of sweet blossom is displayed in a showy celebration of renewal and abundance.

I have been reading a diary about rural life, written in the 1700s, by a country person and churchgoer. In those days, Lent was strictly observed as a time of abstinence, especially from eating meat. But for most people, late winter and early spring were times of hardship, and the consumption of meat was not an option anyway; it was simply not available. Subsistence farming, as it mostly was in those days, followed an age-old pattern. Livestock was fattened from grass during the summer months, and slaughtered in the autumn. Only a few breeding animals were kept alive during the winter, often with great difficulty. Apart from the very wealthy, few could afford to eat meat. For most people, abstinence in Lent was automatic – thus creating a virtue from necessity.

I am sure that many people will have been as concerned as I was to read recently of the government's plans to make changes to our national flag. The Union Jack, or Union Flag as it is otherwise known, has its origins from when King James VI of Scotland also became King of England. England and Wales were already united, and eventually, in 1707, the union of the two realms was accomplished. A new flag was adopted, consisting of the crosses of St George and St Andrew. In 1801, following the union of Ireland with Great Britain, the cross of St Patrick was added, and the design has remained unchanged ever since. For over 200 years, the Union Jack has been recognised throughout the world as a symbol of our national identity.

It has now been decided however, that our flag is to receive a makeover, to reflect a more 'passive' phase in our national development. Apparently, some groups may have been offended by the historical significance of the three crosses of St George, St Andrew and St Patrick, the patron saints of England, Scotland and Ireland respectively. According to the findings of a government think tank, the existing sharp, angular design with its bright primary colours could be seen as 'provocative'. A top PR company has been paid an undisclosed sum of money to produce a re-vamped version, which has already received government approval. The familiar hard lines are to be softened, giving the impression that the three crosses are merging together, and the distinctive red, white and blue is to be replaced by pastel shades of pink, yellow and grey, thus avoiding the 'exclusive' and 'individualist' images of the past. What I find most unacceptable is the undue haste with which these changes are to be implemented. Thousands of new flags have already been made, and are to be hoisted on public buildings from 1st April, by which time all old flags are to be removed.

April 2009

Floodwater and Blossom

After four long months of predominantly wet and windy conditions, rapid changes have come lately in both the weather and the countryside. The winter, although mild, brought the highest rainfall for many years, and by the middle of March 41 inches of rain had fallen in the district since last July. (Our annual average is about 27 inches.) The river and surrounding meadows here have been flooded many times during the winter, but the biggest floods came on 6th March. Our sheep, which had been grazing a low-lying meadow, were in danger of being marooned by rising floodwater. We had great difficulty trying to coax the little flock over a culvert, already covered by about a foot of water, in order to move them on to higher ground. Two days later I was in my shirtsleeves on a warm sunny afternoon pruning some young trees in a spinney, when I came across a patch of coltsfoot in bloom, the bright orangy-yellow flowers confirming that spring had arrived at last. There is always some definite point each year when one instinctively knows that winter has passed and cannot return, and if another cold spell comes it will not last long.

On the following Sunday we visited friends in the Cambridgeshire village of Hemingford Grey. After lunch a group of us walked the short distance to St Ives, through a large flat and soggy meadow adjacent to the Great Ouse, still swollen with muddy water. I remarked that we had seen some of this water the day before – flowing through our own farm! A couple of days later another friend had kindly invited me racing on the first day of the Cheltenham Festival. We enjoyed the drive through the picturesque Cotswold landscape on a perfect spring morning, many of the gardens along the way displaying pink and white blossoms of early-flowering prunus. On the drier, brashy limestone hills we saw land being cultivated and drilled. The going was good at Cheltenham; the racecourse, billed as the home of National Hunt Racing, is in a wonderfully scenic position and lies in what is virtually a natural amphitheatre. The sun shone continuously and I enjoyed my day away from the farm. The following day my own fields had dried enough to allow me to catch up with some crop spraying; this was the first opportunity to get out on to the land since early November, and only a week after the sheep had been stranded by floods. The soil was still tender in places however, and I was grateful for my flotation tyres. It felt good to be out in the fields again, and I saw several pheasants and young leverets running about in the wheat.

There have been plenty of signs announcing the arrival of spring. The violets and primroses of early March are already past their best, and hazel catkins have shed their pollen and become old and dry. Spring seems earlier than usual this year; I'm sure that the hellebores, euphorbia and amelanchier in our garden are a week ahead of last year, this progress could soon be halted however. There are many set-backs on the road from winter to spring, and the blackthorn is yet to flower fully. We normally suffer a cold spell when it does, and the 'Blackthorn Winter' usually occurs around the time of the spring equinox and often lasts into April, the main month of spring and the one which brings the greatest change of all. Bare, wintry branches at the beginning of the month will be flushed with new leaf by the end, and the clouds of icy-white blackthorn blossom which adorn the hedgerows in the first few days of April will be replaced by the dreamy fragrance of hawthorn flowers by early May. Much is displayed before our eyes, fresh creation is revealed each day, from cowslips and wood anemones to bluebells and cherry blossom, from sticky buds to horse chestnut candles. Swallows arrive and the cuckoo sings; so many changes unveiled in the space of a month. Winter has had its day: spring is now firmly in control.

March 2007

A Spring Survey

The wind was high and roaring in the trees on a bright spring day; the fields and woods seemed thrillingly wild and vibrant again after the long winter. I was out cultivating ploughed land in preparation for planting spring crops. I turned on the field headland, and a hare sprang from its shallow form on the ground, only a few feet from the tractor. His black tipped ears instantly became erect, and his long hind legs propelled him away over the bare soil with the speed of a greyhound. Hares are handsome creatures; it is always a pleasant surprise to see one, but within minutes I saw three more now all racing around and cavorting with each other, clearly in high spirits in this their breeding season. Later, when moving on to the next field, I drove up a grassy track alongside one of our spinneys. As I climbed down from the tractor to open the gate my eye was taken by a swathe of white blossom at ground level in amongst the trees, made brighter at that moment by sunshine filtering down through the branches. The wood anemones were beginning to flower again, and I could not resist walking the few paces into the spinney to admire them. As I did so I disturbed a buzzard which took off from the top of a sycamore; other birds were immediately alerted to my presence. In a brief flurry of activity a woodcock rose from the under-storey in a low, swinging flight, and I heard a mixture of sharp high-pitched birdsong all around me as the alarm was raised.

Last year a very pleasant retired gentleman visited us once in each of the months of April, May and June. He always chose fine weather, and arrived about half an hour before dawn; his June visit started at four in the morning. He was an RSPB volunteer whom we had invited to carry out a survey of wild birds on the farm. Identification was achieved by sight, song and behaviour. We already knew that we were lucky enough to have a wide range of birds here, including skylarks, yellowhammers and starlings, all of which are on the RSPB's 'Red' or endangered list, but the survey results confirmed that reed buntings and tree sparrows also live on the farm.

Reed buntings look similar to finches but are less agile and do not flock together, preferring to stay alone or in small groups of two or three. Their simple song is short and repetitive, whilst finches are more musically creative. Reed buntings were found, as you might expect, down by the river in a marshy meadow. They perch on tall bank-side plants rather than up in the trees, and build their nests quite low to the ground, typically hidden and suspended in a thicket of reeds around which the nest is carefully woven. Tree sparrows are quite shy, and are smaller and plumper than house sparrows. They prefer the peace and quiet of remote fields and open woodlands where they tend to nest in holes found in old trees, but will sometimes make their homes in the bases of larger nests belonging to crows or herons; the owners seem happy to accommodate these little interlopers.

Sadly, things are not all positive. In the last two seasons we have hardly seen any lapwings, and this concurs with RSPB findings that we are not alone. Other ground-nesting birds like grey partridges and skylarks are now also in danger, and the blame is often laid at the door of modern farming methods. Those of us who live and work on the land know that the real reasons have more to do with large increases in the numbers of predators than anything else. Some conservationists are reluctant to acknowledge this fact, for fear of upsetting those who are won over by 'cuddly' TV images.

March 2008

Shepherding

Nowadays, our farming is based around arable cropping and conservation, and we also have a small flock of sheep. At certain times of the year we also keep sheep for another farmer; his flock of ewes graze our meadows and grassland from late summer until early winter, returning to their home farm for lambing. Spring is the most physically and mentally demanding time of year for sheep farmers; they often work very long hours in uncomfortable conditions, enduring cold weather and lack of sleep. Many ewes will give birth without help, but some will need assistance. Sick ewes, and lambs which need fostering, demand all the skill and patience of even the most experienced shepherd. It is deeply satisfying in a spiritual sense to be involved in the breeding of animals. Assisting with birth and witnessing new life growing up on the farm is very rewarding; I have seen many lambs and calves come into the world, and have fond memories of past lambing times. As children, we bottle-fed orphaned lambs before and after school, and helped with feeding and watering round the lambing pens. It was quite usual to come home and walk into the kitchen to find a hypothermic lamb reviving in a cardboard box by the Rayburn. Occasionally, critical cases would actually be placed inside the warming oven for a short while, to speed revival! My mother would be called upon for assistance at lambing time – her smaller hands and midwifery skills were invaluable during difficult births. My father sometimes removed the skin from a dead lamb and tied it around an orphan; this would assist in fostering by deceiving a ewe who had lost her own lambs into thinking that the orphan belonged to her.

Very early one Easter Sunday morning, when I was eleven years old, my father and I set off in the car to Radclive, where we had some land. It was just getting light as we arrived at a field of pasture containing a flock of tegs (female sheep in their second year). Most were heavy in lamb, and the little flock needed to be brought home to a more sheltered field, especially as wet weather was forecast. My dad's faithful collie, Mist, gently rounded them up and we counted 140 as they filed steadily out through the field gateway and into the street. I set off walking in front, over the bridge, up the hill and out of the village, with Mist coaxing the sheep along from behind. Dad followed in his car, occasionally calling instructions to me or the dog. Dawn was breaking as we turned left on to the main road, and the horizon was fiery red as the sun rose behind me. It was a slow journey back to the farm, as we successfully negotiated various gateways and hazards, including the Biddlesden junction and The Robin Hood, the crossroads and the P.O.W. camp, before eventually arriving at the home pasture in Water Stratford. I don't remember seeing a single car on the way – how things have changed!

My father was a stickler for checking livestock numbers, and we stood either side of the half-open gateway counting the sheep again as they ran into the field. The first drops of rain were falling as he closed the gate behind the last few stragglers. "How many?" came the inevitable question, and I had to admit that I had counted only 139. " I think we've lost one…" I suggested nervously. But he was smiling. "Wrong!" he said. "142 is now the correct number!" He opened the back door of the car and there was the missing teg – with two tiny but very noisy lambs. The collie and the new mother were licking one lamb each. The teg had been hanging back from the rest of the flock along the road, and Dad had noticed that her waters had broken. He had caught and lambed her, and simply put the new family into the back of the car and carried on. We put mother and babies into one of the straw-bale shelters at the edge of the field, built a few days earlier in preparation for lambing. It was pouring with rain as we went into the house for a late breakfast of boiled eggs, dyed in various colours (my mother's Easter Sunday speciality) followed by the hurried giving of chocolate Easter eggs – we could not be late for Church.

April 2006

Patience Rewarded

March came blustering in like a lion, and went out like a polar bear. Arctic winds held back the development of grass and grain alike, and early April brought no respite. Snow fell on dates which were, last year, hotter than many days in the summer. By mid April frosty mornings were still commonplace, and we were beginning to wonder how much longer we would be kept waiting for the arrival of spring. We had been philosophical about the floods of February and the bitter blasts of March, but patience was waning. Spring showed her face for a few days in the first half of February, and her smile lifted our spirits, but she soon deserted us again and apart from a few tantalising glimpses we saw little of her for some time. Last year, by contrast, she made a grand entrance in March and we enjoyed her pleasant company until summer arrived, but so far this year, spring has been a very 'yea and nay' affair, to quote Christina Rossetti.

I managed to plant four fields of beans in early March during a short window of opportunity, but other land intended for spring oats was still unfit to work at that time. I have had to be patient; it is no use forcing seed into cold, wet soil. In such circumstances, germination will be delayed and in the meantime, the rooks will help themselves. The old saying 'well sown, half grown' is as true as ever, and the oats were eventually drilled, later than planned, into reasonable seedbeds. The successful sowing of crops is obviously important for financial reasons. But most farmers take pride in their work, and whilst trying to farm efficiently, many strive to produce aesthetically pleasing results as well. Farmers are keenly aware that their fields are constantly on display, and the quality of work may be judged by all. That is why you will usually see the best ploughing, the neatest hedges and the straightest drilling in fields by the road. And it is the scrutiny of fellow farmers which is feared the most! Warm spring weather is now needed to allow us to get on with other seasonal tasks. At present, it is difficult to see how today's relatively bare pastures will provide a crop of hay fit to cut in mid June. By then the beans, which have only just emerged, will be an impenetrable mass of foliage and flowers, and it hardly seems possible that winter wheat crops, now only a few inches high, will produce their first ears by the end of May. How do I know? Trust me – it will all happen according to the annual pattern ordained by nature.

Whilst the coming of spring is a summons to those who work on the land, for everyone else it is a signal to go out and witness the changes the English climate brings to the countryside. Those who walk the footpaths and byways at this glorious time of year are well rewarded. This afternoon a brief shower left a certain rain-fresh smell – the kind that you only experience in spring, and afterwards the dripping hedges either side of the little lane which runs through the farm sparkled in bright sunshine. The wet tarmac shone out, and from a distance the road looked like a carelessly discarded ribbon, winding its way out of Buckinghamshire and over the river into Oxfordshire. But the breeze was still chilly. One day soon the wind, which has been stuck in the north and east for weeks, will find its way round to the west and all will be benign once more. And then there will come a day – and this day usually occurs in early May – when you realise that spring has reached its zenith. On this day there is always such an abundance of exquisite loveliness to be enjoyed, but with it comes the feeling that another year must pass before it will again be possible to experience such precious beauty.

April 2008

Leverets and Wayward Flowers

Opinions differ I know, but I think England shows off her best in May. At no other time of year is one surrounded by such freshness, beauty and promise. Out in the fields the grass and cereal crops are growing fast, but it is still just possible, before plants become tall, to watch hares moving about. Soon there will be too much cover, and we shall no longer be able see them again until after harvest. Female hares have already given birth to litters of two to four young; the leverets were born on the soil surface with a full coat of fur and with their eyes wide open. When a tiny leveret is found alone and apparently vulnerable, it is sometimes assumed that it has been abandoned by its mother. This is not the case; it is normal for the new family to disperse soon after birth, so as to minimise the risk of the whole litter being taken by a predator. Every night and morning for several weeks the mother finds and suckles each baby in turn, before disappearing again. Leverets are appealing, but the temptation to catch one for a cuddle should be resisted: they have sharp teeth.

After almost two years of predominantly wet weather, the long dry spell in early spring was very welcome. During the fine weeks I planted about two hundred acres of beans, spring oats and linseed in fourteen different fields, mostly in reasonable conditions. By the first few days of April clouds of dust were rising from the ring rolls as they went clanking over the fields of freshly drilled linseed, leaving the ribbed surface of the soil looking like corduroy. 'Plant seed in the dust – come it must' my father used to say. And so it was that initial worries about seedbeds drying out were later dispelled by the rains in the second half of the month. Each spring is different, and in some years it is not always possible to roll before seed germinates, because the soil may be too damp, and liable to stick to the iron sections. However, I like to use my ring (or Cambridge) rolls whenever possible, after both spring and autumn planting. Many of our fields are of the limestone brash type of soil with some quite large stones; pressing them down by rolling helps to avoid damage to the combine during harvest, while at the same time ensuring that the seed is firmly in contact with the soil. Some of our stoniest fields are very light in colour after cultivation, and in wet weather the limestone is washed clean by rain. From a distance the bare land looks bleached, like the colour of last year's dead grass.

Before seedbeds were prepared, some weeds were growing on the over-wintered land, and I enjoyed seeing again the tiny sky-blue flowers of speedwell, and the purple and creamy yellows of field pansy. This plant is closely related to wild pansy, also known as heartsease; the flowers are perfect miniatures of their garden cousins. A weed is, after all, only a plant in the wrong place. Earlier in the year snowdrops bloomed along the banks of the stream; the bulbs had probably been transplanted in the past by floods. Elsewhere on the farm periwinkle grows under the edge of a wood, and some honesty seed pods must have been blown several hundred yards away from the house; the rich purple flowers are now showing among the cow parsley on the edge of a wheat field headland. These wayward garden plants are just as welcome in rustic places as they are in herbaceous borders, and are a reminder that nature will always select her own seed. To become reacquainted each year with the familiar scents and colours of flowers, cultivated or wild, is like being reunited with old friends. Every shade, fragrance and characteristic is faithfully reproduced on an annual basis; in a way that is not just similar, nearly, or almost, but exactly the same, year after year.

May 2009

The Drill Wheel

Oh, the trouble that my father had!
I remember it still.
During a spell of dry weather,
The iron tyre worked loose
From a wooden wheel
On our old Smythe drill.
After the long day's sowing,
He took the whole wheel off
And dropped it in the river.
It seemed a doubtful scheme.
Next morning,
Before we could get going,
He slipped the wheel back on.
The wood had swelled throughout the night until
The tyre was held completely tight;
It worked like a dream.
That was when I realised why
The Hay Wain,
Painted by John Constable near Flatford Mill,
Was standing in the stream.

*Note: The Smythe family built their world famous
seed drills at Peasenhall, Suffolk, from 1800 to 1960.*

25

A Kind of Magic

Every spring our collie moults at exactly the right time for the birds, thoughtfully providing soft material for nest building. When her moult is in full swing we take her out onto the lawn and pluck away as much of her old winter coat as possible, so as to minimise the hair that gets shed inside the house with the potential to block the vacuum cleaner. Dog hair blows around the garden, but is gone within a few hours. Quite recently I noticed that a small tuft of her hair had appeared, as if by magic, sticking out from a hole high up on the garden wall: the flycatchers were back, building in their usual place. The nests of finches, robins and sparrows close by also contain some of the distinctive black and white hair.

The collie is usually quite a good guard dog, but she did not detect an early morning visitor we had last week. Part of the garden merges almost seamlessly with the surrounding fields, and other than a dry ditch there is no definite boundary. This is a characteristic that I have sought to create – I like the way that the lawn blends into the landscape. There is a price to pay however, in that we have to share our garden with more of the local wildlife than is perhaps good for us. From time to time holes caused by badgers searching for earthworms appear in the lawn and flowers are occasionally eaten off by rabbits. These are the annoying consequences of the open situation, but are just about acceptable when offset by the pleasure of seeing a hare running across the grass or a stoat bounding amongst the shrubs, with its distinctive hump-backed gait, stopping to satisfy its curiosity as it glances out from a border. In any case I like to enjoy the view over the fields, uninterrupted by fence or hedge.

I was up before sunrise the other morning, and just as it was getting light I stood at the bedroom window and gazed out across the lawn. The air was thick with early morning mist and I could see nothing beyond the garden. Suddenly an image materialised and there, standing like a statue at the far end of the lawn, half obscured by vapour, was a muntjac. I stayed motionless, never taking my eyes off the deer for a second, and then, in an instant it was gone. I did not see it come, and I did not see it go. I was so surprised that I started to doubt whether the deer had been there at all – was it some apparition, the work of an unseen conjuror? Muntjac are smaller and less elegant than other deer, looking a bit like long-legged pigs. They are also known as 'barking deer', because of their cries, but this name is appropriate for another reason. I knew I had not been mistaken that morning when we later found that the bark had been stripped from two eucalyptus trees, a young plum tree and a golden willow. A newly planted whitebeam had also been damaged; its fresh buds had all been nipped off. I have fitted spiral guards on my smaller trees to protect them from rabbits, but they are no defence against deer. The antlers of the male muntjac are short and stubby, and are covered in soft skin known as velvet which becomes itchy at this time of year. Deer often rub their antlers against saplings to relieve the irritation, whilst at the same time scent-marking their territory, typically standing on their hind legs to do so. The result is usually frayed bark and lower branches broken.

I have also suffered damage from wildlife out in the fields lately, with wood pigeons grazing my crops. It can be difficult to deter them once they get used to feeding in certain fields. A few years ago I made some scarecrows consisting of plywood cut-outs of a man aiming a shotgun; these were mounted on a steel spindles which can be pushed into the ground, allowing the men to swivel in the wind. I painted the men in different colours and styles, and I swear that one of them looks a bit like Paul Daniels. I've been using a gas banger to try to keep pigeons off my pea crop, but inevitably they get used to the bangs after a while and this method becomes ineffective. Eventually I replaced the banger with some swivelling men; I placed them in various positions in two of my pea fields, with Paul in charge of a corner by a wood. After a few days, the pigeons seemed to be leaving this area alone, and with some showers and warmer weather the peas have now recovered. Magic.

May 2005

Attention Deficit

In early spring, when traces of winter are still evident and the hardships of the cold and wet are fresh in the memory, we want to speed things along to the kinder months. But now is the time when we would like to slow down the passing of the season; as May gives way to June we would apply the brake, if only we could, to allow us the time to take in all the wonders around us. The annual transformation of trees and plants, which happens in just a few short weeks, is amazing. The change in the hedgerows from the wintery browns of bare branches to the green shades of spring occurs almost overnight. Now, as you drive along the lanes you feel as though you could almost reach out and touch the delicious softness of the fresh tresses of leaves, cascading from hedges fragrant with sweet, vanilla-like hawthorn blossom.

I meant to go back and take a closer look at a crab tree in full bloom in the corner of a field, half glimpsed as I passed by on a tractor. Just last week it was attended by bumble bees, but I'm already too late – the blossom is over. A great deal is happening now, and no matter how attentive I am, I inevitably miss so much at this busy time of year. Spring and summer demand my attention to both farm and garden; the farm always takes precedence of course, but it is important that our garden is developed and maintained to provide enjoyment for our paying guests, as well as for ourselves. On many evenings this spring there have been desperate attempts to catch up with gardening jobs. My first priority was to plant out all the container grown shrubs that have been hanging about since autumn. (We never quite get everything planted before our enthusiasm compels us to rush out and buy yet more plants!) However, I was soon distracted when other more pressing tasks became urgent. For example, we found some tulip bulbs in the greenhouse, still in their bag, which we had bought in October, and then completely forgotten about. They were hastily planted at the end of March, in hope rather than optimism, but they flowered beautifully in mid May, only a couple of weeks after the November planted ones.

The hours seem to melt away when gardening, and I never have enough time to finish all the jobs. I like visiting other gardens, but rarely get the opportunity to do so. However, we did go to Evenley Wood Garden at the end of April. I used to farm the land along Mill Lane, so I am familiar with this sixty acre wood, which Mr & Mrs R T Whiteley purchased in the early 1980s. In the last twenty-five years they have transformed about half of it from what was a fairly ordinary and neglected old conifer and broadleaved plantation into a magnificent woodland garden. Good use has been made of the undulating land, which falls gently down to the banks of a little stream, to display a wide variety of fine ornamental trees, shrubs, bulbs and wild flowers. The careful attention to detail, both when selecting plants and choosing the best sites, is self-evident.There are over three thousand varieties, consisting of single specimen trees, groups of shrubs and dramatic swathes of flowering plants. A broad band of acid soil, untypical of the district, lies under about a quarter of the wooded area, and this has provided the opportunity to plant a wonderful collection of rhododendrons, magnolias and camellias. It is almost as if the wood, which offers little clue from the outside of the delights which lie within, contains a miniature landscape garden. Evenley Wood is famous for birdsong, and walking the mown paths and avenues accompanied by birds singing in the trees is a real pleasure. Visits can be arranged for groups of enthusiasts who wish to experience the dawn chorus; however, they must be prepared to arrive before 4.30am.

May 2006

A Peck and a Bite

For a couple of days in the middle of March, after a day's drilling, it would have just about been possible to collect a peck of soil dust from the surfaces of my seed drill's framework. The old English volumetric measure equates to about ten litres, and the traditional saying, 'A peck of March dust is worth a king's ransom', refers to the value of weather dry enough in that month to allow the sowing of seeds. Wind and rain soon returned to lay the dust, but thankfully, not before I had planted my bean and oat fields. The new seedlings were just breaking the soil surface on Good Friday. That day was cold, wet and stormy, and on the following morning the dogs were denied their usual swim – it was too dangerous with the river in spate. When we arrived home both of them had to be de-burred; they had collected several adhesive seed-heads from last year's burdock plants by the riverbank. Each marble-sized burr has hundreds of tiny hooked fingers, which attach to the fur of passing animals – a brilliant mechanism for seed dispersal and one which inspired the invention of Velcro.

Spring has been later this year, and by Easter there was still no significant new growth of grass on the pastures. Ewes with young lambs at foot need fresh grazing to keep up their milk supply, and farmers with dairy cows or beef cattle were hoping for an early bite of spring grass following the interminable winter, so that livestock could be turned out to pasture after many months confined to cattle yards. Supplies of hay and straw become scarce after a hard winter; the day of turn-out brings huge relief to both man and beast. The farmer's work-load is cut at a stroke – all the time spent, seven days a week from late autumn throughout the winter, feeding, bedding and tending to the general needs of housed livestock is now saved – once the animals are outside again he need only spend a short time each day walking round checking his stock, leaving several hours free for other farming jobs which become urgent in spring. And the cost of keeping livestock at pasture is a mere fraction of the expensive business of artificial feeding and bedding inside buildings during the long months of winter.

The spectacle of cattle being released from their winter quarters and turned out to grass in springtime is greatly entertaining. At first, they are reluctant to leave the familiar surroundings of the covered yard; one or two might come out initially, but they are nervous and easily spooked by unfamiliar smells and views. The light is much brighter outside than in the buildings, and it takes time for the cattle to become accustomed. The first ones out often run straight back in again, and the whole bunch becomes frisky; they sense that something unusual is happening. Even when finally out in the field, they are unable to graze for an hour or two – there is too much excitement and joy at their new-found freedom. They can feel the sun on their backs, the fresh air intoxicates them, and plenty of hollering and bellowing occurs together with much sniffing and snorting. The odd mouthful of grass is snatched between bouts of cavorting and galloping around; heels are kicked in the air in sheer ecstasy at the sights and scents of spring. During the next couple of hours more grass will be trampled than eaten; eventually the cattle are out of breath and sweaty with all the running around exploring their new surroundings. By the next morning they will have settled down; the farmer will go to check and find them lying peacefully together, chewing the cud and looking forward to more of that lovely May grass. Gentle, kind eyes follow his every move. The cattle are quiet and contented now, their bellies are full and they have already forgotten the confinement of the last six months.

May 2010

Summer

Buzzers and Bells

The coarse fishing season does not begin until June 16th, but trout will soon be rising to the first mayfly hatch of the year. A couple of friends visited us in mid May for a bit of fly fishing, during a calm and sunny spell of weather. Sit quietly on the riverbank on a warm day in late spring, and the effects of watching insects buzzing over the water can be quite soporific. But for the creatures themselves, life is anything but sleepy. Many of them are newly hatched, and they feed with some urgency in order to grow and gain enough strength to breed before their short lives are over. The slower-moving stretches of river are generally favoured by most insects; the ones with long legs make use of the surface tension for support thus allowing them to skate rapidly across the water in search of food, or to escape predators.

Damselflies and dragonflies are common on the river, especially the blue damselfly, which is usually present in reasonable numbers by mid summer. They skim along, inches above the surface, rising to dance in the air under the bank-side trees before landing on rushes or taller grasses. Damselflies stay near the river margins, basking in the sun, displaying their azure iridescence with wings folded along the length of their bodies. Some types do not gain their adult colours until they have eaten their first meal. Occasionally you see them in the mating position: mature couples joined together, head to tail and tail to head in a distinctive heart-shaped union. Dragonflies, unlike the smaller damselflies, hold their four delicate wings of fine gauze out straight when settled. They are masters of aerobatics, able to hover, fly backwards or even upside down; they also have compound eyes which allow nearly 360 degrees of vision, making them formidable predators. The emperor is the largest of the dragonflies; I once found a dead one in a wood – they do not always stay close to the river – it was in perfect condition, and I was able to study its beautiful body closely.

The weather and ground conditions back in mid April were perfect for planting, and during three days of frantic activity we drilled all our spring crops. The rain came right on cue just after the last field had been rolled, and a poem came to mind: 'Sowing', by Edward Thomas. In two of the fields we planted spring rape to replace the winter rape which had failed; it is always difficult to judge where to 'draw the line' when faced with thin, patchy crops, and I now wish I had scrapped other fields of poorly established rape. Four fields were planted with peas, which are a good break crop from wheat because, being a legume, they leave a little nitrogen in the soil. During flowering, peas and beans are attractive to bees, nature's miracle workers, who perform the dual services of pollinating the crop for the farmer and producing honey for the beekeeper. We drilled linseed in the remaining fields. How this crop, which appears so innocently fragile in June with its shy, delicate lilac-blue flowers on slender stems, can become such a menace at harvest time I do not know. By then its stalks are as strong as fencing wire and refuse to be cut unless they are completely dead and the sun is shining brightly. Timing is everything in farming – it has been said that the difference between a good farmer and a bad one is about two weeks. But there is never any set time for husbandry tasks, everything always depends on the weather and we only have the benefit of hindsight with which to judge whether we have made the best use of opportunities. It turns out that I picked the last dry spell in the spring for my planting.

Recently, during a rare break from work, we spent a pleasant afternoon visiting the gardens at Coton Manor near Guilsborough. For me the best part was the magnificent Bluebell Wood. Words fail to describe the beauty that lay beneath the tall beech and hornbeam trees whose new and unblemished leaves are at their best now, before they darken as the season unfolds. The dappled sunlight shining through the pale green foliage enhanced the swathes of bluebells in a kind of ethereal way, reminding me that this is my favourite time of year; much is happening now, but there remains the promise of so much more to come. And now the pageant of spring and early summer continues into the fragrant month of June, with the essential ingredients of warmth and moisture, sunlight and shade promoting growth and regeneration; each day revealing new delights which, although happen every year, still manage to take us by surprise.

May 2004

Raiders of Stream and Garden

On a beautiful evening in May, all was bathed in golden sunlight; the breeze gently stirred the newly emerged leaves, lovely and fresh in their many shades of green. In the paddock beyond the garden the ewes were suckling their young lambs while two magpies hopped about in the grass. The weather was settled, and the following morning was again fine. Just after sunrise the dawn chorus was interrupted by a shrill high-pitched squawking, followed by a brief silence, before birdsong resumed as before. As I crossed the lawn a couple of hours later, I noticed some broken eggshell on the ground, pale blue with black spots. I immediately checked the honeysuckle where I knew there was a song thrush's nest. Sure enough it had been raided and the empty nest was now deserted. Looking up I saw a magpie fly out of the top of the big ash tree at the end of the garden, and away over the hedge beyond.

The little stream which runs through our fields is overhung on either side with trees of ash and oak, alder, crab and willow, interspersed with clumps of field maple and thorn, the overgrown relics of former hedges. Now that the leaves are fully out and the bank-side vegetation is lush, the water has become mostly hidden from view. It flows through our land in a gully before joining the river, overhead branches coming together to form a kind of tunnel. On climbing down the bank you enter a cooler, darker world, the peaceful sound of running water broken occasionally perhaps by the cackle of a pheasant or a pair of startled mallards suddenly taking flight. The sunlight penetrates the leafy canopy in places, illuminating the stony bed of the stream, the surface of the water catching the light as it ripples away. Once or twice I have seen a brown trout here, but there is not enough water to sustain many fish, especially in the dry summer months. However, not for nothing does a heron sometimes loiter here – I have no doubt that herons take fish from the stream. They are opportunists and will also eat crayfish, frogs, toads and small mammals such as shrews and even water voles. They are strange-looking birds and seem as though they belong to the age of dinosaurs with their snake-like neck and fearsome beak with which they stab their prey. Even in flight, the slow, lazy wing beat and cocked-back head gives them a prehistoric appearance. The stream joins the river a little further on; the river bed is now much cleaner than it was last year. All the accumulated debris and dead plant material has been washed away by the winter floods; the river will now be healthier in the months to come. The rain stopped abruptly in March, and two dry months passed by. I don't remember another April without April showers, but nature, as always, had restored the balance with the rains of mid May. Strange how wet weather, no matter how badly needed, soon becomes a nuisance.

The warm, dry spring must have encouraged more bird activity than usual, or at any rate, birds seem to have been easier to spot. This was certainly the case along the river, where further downstream a pair of kingfishers nested. The kingfisher must be one of our most beautiful birds; it is such a treat to see their turquoise blue and bright orange plumage, even for a split second as one zips by, but better still if you are lucky enough to see one sitting motionless on an overhanging branch, just above the surface of a still pool. Kingfishers are probably benefiting from climate change; in the past large numbers have been known to perish during very cold, icy winters. I wish moorhens would return to our stretch of the river; they were common twenty or thirty years ago, but have been preyed upon by mink, which take their eggs and will also kill adult birds. Back in the garden a family of blue tits have just fledged from their nest in a blackthorn bush. As far as I could tell there were five youngsters being shepherded around by their parents as they flitted along the branches of a maple. Meanwhile, somewhere in a nearby thicket a lonely song thrush silently mourned the loss of her family.

May 2007

The Plight of the Honey Bee

They say that summer does not really begin until the elder blossom comes, and has ended by the time the berries are fully ripe. June is the first proper summer month, during which our national flower, the wild rose, appears. The English rose is probably the most beloved of all the flowers of the countryside, and one of the last to bloom in the hedgerows. It does not stay for long, and is among many of the delights that should be enjoyed on the journey through summer, when the travelling is more enjoyable than the arrival. June's blossoms are the sweetest of the year; the hedges especially are magnificent just now, elderflower, dog rose, privet and wild honeysuckle all adding to the heady mix of scented air, further enhanced by warm sunshine. These summer fragrances are lovely, but they have not been provided solely for our benefit. Their purpose is to attract pollinating insects to help plants with the task of fertilisation, without which reproduction and the formation of fruit and seed could not take place.

My spring planted crops of beans have established well, and I am looking forward to the flowering period when their distinctive scent wafts over the fields in the early evenings, after hot June days. The linseed too, will be flowering around the same time. At this time of year, given fine weather, one would normally expect these crops to be humming with the sound of bees, and I sincerely hope that they will be. But, like many farmers, I am becoming increasingly concerned about reports regarding the decline of the honey bee. Bees are vital to agriculture and horticulture, helping to pollinate many different types of crops, whilst at the same time producing honey from nectar. In fact one third of the world's food production is largely dependent on bees. And now there is a shortage of honey because in the UK we can no longer produce enough to satisfy demand, and so greater supplies are being obtained from overseas. However, imported honey sometimes contains bacteria that is harmful to our bees; there is a risk that they may, for example, feed on honey remaining in a discarded jar, become infected, and in turn infect the rest of their colony.

Apparently, since 2006, thirty per cent of the bee population has disappeared. This situation has mostly been caused by the mysterious failure of adult worker bees to be able to find their way back to their hives. The larvae and queen, having therefore been abandoned, cannot survive and soon die.

This phenomenon is now officially known as Colony Collapse Disorder (CCD). No-one yet knows the causes, but various theories have been suggested, such as radiation from power cables or mobile phone masts interfering with the navigation systems of bees. Diseases like foul brood have always been a threat, because the high density of bee populations is ideal for the spread of infection, and the wet summers of 2007 and 2008 must also have contributed to high rates of mortality in the UK. For the last twenty years or so, a more serious threat has been present in the shape of a parasite known as the varroa mite, which carries a deadly virus. Varroa can be controlled by chemicals, but success is not always guaranteed. CCD, however, is totally devastating to affected colonies, and there is no known way of preventing it. This is all quite depressing and unless solutions can be quickly discovered, the demise of the honey bee is an alarming possibility which could have a profound effect on our future diet. One single hive of sixty thousand bees is capable of pollinating half a million plants a day; it is difficult to see how this could be achieved in the absence of bees. A quote which is often attributed to Albert Einstein claims, "If bees were to become extinct, mankind would only survive for a further four years".

June 2009

The Organic Debate

Last year I grew crops of phacelia (see front cover) and clover on fields which, under Defra regulations, I was obliged to set aside from normal arable cropping. The intention was to maintain good soil health whilst this land was out of production; these cover crops were ploughed in during August, at the end of the 'set aside' period. However, the sight of them prompted people to ask if I was 'going organic' – the short answer is no, but I have a problem here with definition. According to most dictionaries, the word organic means 'derived from living matter' or 'of natural development'. The label 'organic farming' therefore implies that non organic farming must be unnatural, which of course is nonsense: all farming is unnatural; it is in conflict with nature. There is precious little about the countryside that is natural. Hedges, for instance, are unnatural: they exist as a result of Acts of Parliament, passed hundreds of years ago, which decreed that land must be enclosed. The countryside has been shaped by countless generations and has become multi-functional, providing food, timber, minerals and water, and a home for native flora and fauna. It also provides amenity, and is the place where power is generated and waste is disposed of; it has not been natural for thousands of years. Organic farming's claim to be 'natural' is therefore misleading, and the one sided picture painted by organic PR, successful though it has been in promoting its products, seeks to discredit conventional farming by propaganda and false claims.

Consumers, however, must have choice, and their right to choose organic is not questioned, but they should be making informed choices. Most people think that 'organic' means 'no chemicals', but organic farmers are allowed to use certain pesticides, and their crops take up to twice the amount of energy to grow as conventional crops, occupying more land to grow less food, which is wasteful of resources and bad for the environment. Standards of organic farming vary according to country of origin; much of the organic food consumed in the UK is imported, with obvious implications in terms of 'food miles'. There is no evidence that organic food is safer or more nutritious than conventionally grown food; permitted levels of pesticide residue in UK food are about one thousand times lower than the accepted safe levels for human consumption anyway, so all home-produced food is extremely safe in terms of residues. Neither are there any particular benefits to wildlife from organic methods; in fact some practices, like the repeated use of harrows on crops and grass in springtime for example, are hostile to ground nesting birds, insects and small mammals.

'Organic' is really the farming of yesterday; it accounts for less than five per cent of the total area farmed in the UK, and much of that is grassland. It is simply not possible for organic farming to deliver quality food in sufficient quantity for our needs – there just isn't enough land. There will always be a niche market for organic food in the wealthiest nations, but it will never feed a hungry world. Modern crop protection systems have enabled conventional farmers to double yields of many crops since the Second World War; we should be proud of this success story, not defensive about it. Pressure on land use is likely to increase in future because of climate change and the need to generate power from non fossil fuel. If we want to grow quality high-yielding crops which need less water on limited areas of land, and at the same time almost eliminate the need for pesticides, perhaps we should look again at the technology of genetic modification, which offers many benefits, but so far has had a very bad press because the government has mishandled the whole issue. There is nothing new about GM. By selective breeding of plants and animals, man has been genetically modifying for thousands of years; modern science could now accelerate the process with great advantage to all, provided it is properly controlled.

June 2007

The Drove Road

Early one June morning I was driving from Biddlesden past Wood Green towards the Stowe road, when I noticed some wild honeysuckle growing in the hedge opposite a wooded stretch known as Coopers Ridings. I pulled over to take a closer look; the road at this point was still in the shadow of the trees but the sun was already strong. I was struck by the stillness of the fresh summer morning on this quiet back road, and I remembered that I was standing on an ancient highway, The Welsh Lane – an old cattle drovers' road. The practice of driving cattle from Wales to the Midlands and on to London first began in the Middle Ages. Cattle reared in North Wales were collected into groups at the Welsh border near Wrexham, and were driven into England via Shropshire and on through the counties of Warwickshire, Northamptonshire and Buckinghamshire to London, in herds of between fifty and one hundred head. The journey would have taken several weeks, averaging about five to ten miles per day, depending on the weather and the conditions of the roads. The unmetalled surfaces would have been rough in winter, uneven with stones and mud packed hard by the tread of people and animals, and often treacherous when the potholes and ruts from cartwheels were full of water and sometimes frozen.

The route probably varied over the centuries – the drovers would have been keen to avoid toll roads for economic reasons, and the advent of parliamentary enclosure would have also influenced their choice of way. Small hedged pasture fields by the roadside known as 'stances' were used for holding cattle during overnight stops. Eventually a well-trodden route was established which became known as the Welsh Lane. From the Midlands through Kenilworth, Southam and Culworth, the drovers came to Sulgrave and Syresham through Biddlesden and on to Buckingham, crossing the Watersplash at Boycott Farm. The little stream runs over the road here, and no doubt provided a welcome drink and a cooling off for hot and aching feet. The cattle were driven onwards to Winslow, Whitchurch and Aylesbury before eventually reaching London. Numbers of Welsh cattle driven to England gradually increased until the 1800s when over seventy thousand head were sold annually at the famous Smithfield meat market. The drovers must have been tough but trustworthy characters; they were responsible for selling the cattle at the end of their journey and delivering the money safely to the owners. Highway robbery was common and by devising a system to avoid theft of cash, drovers were probably among the first people to develop arrangements leading to the early stages of banking. Not all the cattle went as far as London; many were sold at the major Midland cattle markets of Banbury and Northampton, and some at the smaller markets of Buckingham, Winslow and Aylesbury. These were often the younger or store cattle, which would be fattened on the richer pastures of the Midlands and the Home Counties.

By stopping briefly on that early summer morning and thinking about the past, I felt that I was in some way acknowledging the hidden spirits of the drovers who passed through here with their cattle hundreds of years ago. I gazed along the road trying to imagine what this scene would have been like in those days. Today, the roadside hedges were dotted with elderflower and wild rose, and the verges, as yet uncut, were high with hogweed in full flower and cow parsley, almost over and going to seed. There were tall grasses of cocksfoot, bent and annual meadow grass, with Yorkshire fog in damper areas. Within a few hundred yards early poppies and the last of the yellow hawkbit were flowering together in a colourful contrast of reds and yellows, and bird's foot trefoil, bladder campion and moon daisies were also making a show, adding to the rich mixture of colours. It is rare nowadays to see livestock being driven along the roads in this part of the country, even for short distances. Volume of traffic and motorists' intolerance have discouraged the practice. Long distance cattle droving by way of this peaceful lane which is so familiar to us today, died out when the railways came. For a hundred years cattle were moved across the country by train, but that mode of transport also came to an end in time; cattle lorries and livestock trailers do the work today.

June 2005

A Snapshot of Summer

The cuckoo has become silent, the bluebells collapsed weeks ago and it is no longer possible to see the patches in the lawn where the daffodils once were. The mid morning sun is strong on this last Saturday in June, and the English summer is in full swing. Wimbledon fortnight is half way through and it is Glastonbury Festival time. The Lions are playing South Africa in the second test, and the papers are full of the death of Michael Jackson. For us, this weekend is in quiet contrast to last, with all its demands concerning accommodation for the Grand Prix, and farm work is, for once, up to date. In any case, this is day three of recovery following my hernia operation, and I am still feeling a little delicate.

Forced relaxation causes me to have been driven to Brackley; the intention is to search for a wedding present in the Antique Cellar, but we are distracted by live music being played outside the Town Hall. We sit with thirty or forty others in the cobbled square, and enjoy some very pleasant folk and rock music, part of the Brackley Summer Festival. The amplifiers have just enough volume to overcome the traffic noise and pervade the nearby shops. There is a great atmosphere in the town today, but the noonday sun is now quite hot so after a few more numbers we walk over to a favourite haunt: the Old Hall Bookshop. We spend an hour browsing the second hand books in the relative cool of the shop, while still able to enjoy the music coming from the square. Presently we make a couple of purchases and as we are leaving, quite by chance we meet an old friend and catch up with his news.

It is after 2pm by now, so we decide to give the Antique Cellar a miss. After a brief visit to Waitrose, we drive home for a late alfresco lunch, under the shade of an apple tree. The lawn was only cut on Tuesday, but already the white clover has, as if by magic, somehow produced a fresh drift of flowers, which now attract the attention of bumble bees, and their gentle hum adds to the miscellany of summer sounds in the garden. It is definitely an 'Adlestrop' afternoon, and coincidentally, Edward Thomas and Vita Sackville-West are the two authors I bought earlier. Late June, and yes, there are high cloudlets in the sky; a blackbird sings, and we hear the various responses – sharp, clear birdsong from the edge of the garden, then coming more softly from the nearby trees, and finally a faint mixture of song drifts from the fields and the hazy distance beyond, and I know exactly what was experienced on that railway platform a hundred years ago. The sleepy drone of an old biplane overhead, apparently making its way to Turweston Airfield, adds to the timelessness of this quintessentially English summer's day.

We settle down to read – gardens and poetry seem to embrace each other so naturally – but we are soon interrupted by the arrival of another friend who has brought her two young daughters to see us. The three of us chat while the girls play with Molly, our nine-month-old sheepdog. They have really come to see the horses, so we walk over to the stableyard. Routines have been reversed because of the hot weather: the horses are now kept in their stables during the day in an attempt to avoid the flies, and turned out to pasture in the late afternoons. In the end, the Lions give the rugby away in the last minute of the game, but Murray comfortably wins his third round match. Now I am looking forward to watching some of Glastonbury on TV.

June 2009

Butterflies and Grass

For as long as I can remember, every summer orange hawkbit has appeared in the churchyard. I have never noticed it growing anywhere else, and have always thought of it as one of the more uncommon of our native wild flowers, but early in June I was pleasantly surprised to find a patch of it here on the farm in a partly shaded piece of woodland, blooming amongst some young oaks and alders. The bright flame-coloured flowers have a pleasant scent reminiscent of wallflowers, and are borne in clusters on long stems covered in dark hairs. This interesting plant is known by at least two other names: fox and cubs, and, most curiously, grim the collier. Something else exciting happened at the beginning of June – the farm was invaded by painted ladies! I am talking about butterflies of course, migrants from as far away as North Africa, arriving this year for some reason in far greater numbers than usual. It seems entirely appropriate that butterflies should possess some of the most romantic names in the world of wildlife; they add such artistry to nature, looking as they do like flying samples of rare tapestry or fine embroidery.

Since early spring we have seen most of the common butterflies here, including brimstone, large white, hedge brown or gatekeeper, small tortoiseshell, orange tip and red admiral. It has been quite reassuring to see that some species, at least, seem not to have suffered too much from last year's wet breeding season after all. We are certain to see peacocks, large whites and red admirals on the buddleia when it blooms, and marbled whites can always be found feeding on yarrow which flowers in profusion on the site of the old Fulwell and Westbury railway station in July. By mid summer, meadow brown, ringlet, small heath and speckled wood butterflies have usually appeared; ringlets are fond of the bramble growing near the taller hedges and trees which divide our meadows. In spite of last year's wet weather, for several weeks we saw drifts of common blues during sunny intervals, right up until the end of September, along a grassy track which is flanked by patches of white clover. The brown hairstreak and small copper are often more in evidence in late summer and early autumn; they seem to like foraging near ash trees. In previous seasons I have noticed them still flying when we are planting winter wheat in September and early October.

Grasses, too, have interesting names, and as flowering plants are sometimes overlooked, but you need to look closely to appreciate their beauty – there are few things more delicate than the flower of grass. Meadow foxtail is one of the first to seed, followed by the taller, more distinctive cocksfoot. Common bent, smooth and roughstalk meadowgrass and various types of fescue are all open-flowered, but both timothy and crested dogstail produce a single cigar-shaped head, tightly packed with seed. By the middle of June, field margins, grassy banks and any uncut verges show fine displays in various mixtures, often consisting of tall fescue, creeping bent, cocksfoot, soft brome and wall barley, but old hay meadows are the best places to see a wide variety of grasses in flower, just before the mower arrives. A small amount of sweet vernal grows in one of our river meadows – it flowers early and I love the herb-like scent which this grass possesses – it is known as coumarin, and is the reason why hay from this land always smells so sweet. Sterile brome and blackgrass, on the other hand, are regarded as pernicious grass weeds of arable land, and yorkshire fog is undesirable in productive pastures. But a meadow full of yorkshire fog in flower can look quite dreamy, especially on a misty early morning in July, when the whole field seems to have turned purple.

July 2009

A Birthday Wedding

In late July
The season, at a slower pace, allows
Time for romance.
The fragrances of flowers
And second-cut hay
Fill the air with such a rural sweetness,
And in the afternoon
A bride, born on this very day,
Steps out into the street
As high summer's drowsy heat
Pervades the village
For the pageant
Of an English country wedding,
Under a Cotswold sky.

Friends arrive outside the church
And greet each other with a kiss,
They introduce themselves
To cousins staying at The George who say
"Nice to meet you! Lovely day!"
And there is time enough,
Before they're ushered all inside,
To take a photograph
Under the arch
Of the old lychgate.
Then comes the bride
(A little late)
Into the musty coolness
Where no wedding guest can hide
A sudden smile of shy delight
When first they see her,
And older village ladies,
Nodding in agreement, say,
"There's nothing sweeter
Than a pretty summer bride."

Now relaxed, the congregation,
Ceremonial duties over,
Gathers in the churchyard sunshine
Among the gravestones and white clover
The company as sweet at least
As wine which may be gladly sipped
Later, at the wedding feast.
Laughter from the conversation settles
Lightly, on the grass,
As soft as any fallen petals
Of poppy or harebell
Found in nearby lanes and rides,
Along with traveller's joy
Which sprawls about the hedgerows
And above the sides
Of ditch banks, where the wild raspberry grows.
In village gardens plums and cherries hang,
And look – there blooms the buddleia
For all the parish butterflies,
And the happy bride,
Nothing could be lovelier.

Evening sunlight
Brings her special birthday wishes
With glancing golden kisses
On the wheat fields.
They ripen now:
Maturity advancing,
As though compelled by some primeval drum;
The wedding guests, now wined and dined,
Look forward to the dancing,
And many fruitful harvests yet to come.
And though the birds have sung their summer madrigal,
And tides have swept away the cares of youth,
There will be seasons of fair weather left a-plenty,
For seeking future happiness, and truth.

*Written for my sister at the time of her second marriage,
which took place in Gloucestershire in July 2006.*

Ratty

Kenneth Grahame's classic, 'The Wind in the Willows', was published exactly one hundred years ago. The book has been a huge success, and remains among the most charming of children's stories. But I believe that Grahame, no doubt unwittingly, did a disservice to one of his main characters by calling him The Rat. In the book, Ratty was not a rat at all, but a water vole. I suppose Voley would not have had the same ring to it, but unfortunately, some people have inevitably associated him with that despicable creature, the brown rat. Water voles are nothing like rats. They are shy vegetarians, excellent swimmers who live exclusively in the banks of rivers, streams and canals. Much smaller than a rat, they have short furry tails, blunt noses and long whiskery coats. They have undoubtedly suffered a bad press as a result of the confusion, but worse still is the fact that water voles have been preyed upon unmercifully throughout the country for the last forty years by feral mink, almost to the point of extinction.

Mink are devastatingly agile both in and out of the water, and a female mink is slim enough to enter the burrow of a water vole. Water voles have other predators of course, including owls, herons, foxes, stoats and weasels. But these are their natural predators, all indigenous, with whom the water vole once lived in balance, before misguided 'do-gooders' attacked mink farms and released North American mink into the wild. Populations of water voles have since plummeted by around 90%, making it Britain's fastest declining mammal. There was a time when you could not walk along the river bank without hearing several distinct 'plops' as they dived for cover. But now there is new hope for these elusive little creatures, especially along the upper reaches of the Ouse. Captivity-bred water voles are slowly being re-introduced to rivers and streams, but these new colonies will only succeed where the mink population has been reduced, or completely eliminated. After several years of dedicated work involving the control of mink by means of humane live-capture traps, water voles were successfully re-introduced along a stretch of river on a neighbour's farm. A year or so later, we were in contact with Tom, a scientist from the Wildlife Conservation Research Unit at Oxford University, who offered to help us with a similar project on our own farm. The proposed area for re-introduction, a four hundred and fifty metre section of river bank running through one of our meadows, was carefully surveyed.

Water voles feed almost exclusively on aquatic and riverside vegetation; they like wide margins where soft rush, reeds and tussocky grasses grow. Clear, slow-moving water makes an ideal habitat, with steep or stepped banks to accommodate burrows which rise up at an angle, thus keeping above common flood levels. We had already been trapping mink for some time when Tom eventually confirmed that our site was suitable, and one day in May 2007, forty four specially bred water voles arrived. Small family groups were transferred into several release pens which had been prepared beforehand. Handling requires skill, and great care must be taken to avoid being bitten. Tom and his assistant used a Pringle tube to contain each water vole; they are the perfect size for the job. The pens were left intact for a while, providing a refuge for them to return to, if necessary. A few weeks later in July, severe flooding took place over the meadows, giving us cause for concern during this first breeding season. But water voles are prolific breeders, having up to five litters per year, and although further flooding has occurred since, Tom returned last month to check on the new colony and was able to reassure us that all is well and survival rates are good. Provided we can keep mink under control, the water voles, along with other indigenous wildlife such as trout, eels, kingfishers and moorhens, will all once again be able to thrive in relative safety, and The Mole will be reunited with his dear old friend.

July 2008

Cuckoos and Clowns

The national obsession with the weather is such that it is usually the first thing people talk about when they meet. Our weather is mostly unremarkable, and only rarely extreme, but it is the uncertainty of it which fascinates us. Variations sometimes occur between parishes, let alone counties, and we are so conditioned to the local and changeable nature of our weather that during long dry spells we wonder if it will ever rain again, and when it eventually does, we wonder if it will ever stop. Several months of below average rainfall caused a drought in the spring, especially in the South and East, the areas of highest demand for water. Hosepipe bans are still in force in some areas, and today I read that circus clowns in Surrey are forbidden to throw buckets of water over each other during their shows, as this would violate the local drought order. Water pistols have also been banned. Meanwhile, huge volumes of water are lost each day from fractured mains. There are several bursts locally, along the A422 from Buckingham to Brackley; one or two of these have existed not for weeks or months, but for years We currently suffer from several of these leaks; every day thousands of litres of clean, cool drinking water bubble up in some of our fields alongside the main road, flooding areas of crop and leaving the soil waterlogged. We report them time and time again, but rarely is any action taken.

Rainfall during May was about double the average, and by the end of the month the land was wetter than at any time since the autumn. Gardens and farmland were well watered, and even if it doesn't rain again until harvest, the wheat will not suffer. But frequent rain is what our countryside needs; as much as anything else it is the rain which creates the landscape. Rain is falling as I write and the birds are happy, singing away in the trees. The garden echos to the call of a male cuckoo, such a beautiful song from such a despised bird. It occurs to me that there is likely to be a cuckoo's egg in a nearby nest, being hatched by some unsuspecting sparrows or wagtails, along with their own eggs. The life cycle of the cuckoo is entirely dependent on deception. Soon after it has hatched, the cuckoo chick will push everything else out of the nest, and the unwitting foster parents will wear themselves out over the following weeks feeding the cheat which will grow to several times the size of its hosts. By the time the young cuckoo fledges, its biological parents will be long gone. Most birds are taught by their parents about things like diet, habitat, song, migration and so on, but the cuckoo will never see or hear its real parents. Amazingly, it will know instinctively how to fend for itself, and next year it will select and pair with another cuckoo and the whole dishonest process will be repeated.

So now, in the season of the longest days, High Summer begins. More time is spent outside, work ethic diminishes and life in general has an altogether slower rhythm. Well, maybe not for farmers; there is haymaking and harvest to deal with. In June, a traditional hay meadow is a natural garden, full of life and colour with its rich variety of grasses, wild flowers, butterflies and insects. We will cut our meadows in late June or early July, when ground nesting birds have all fledged. The mature grass will be less sappy then, and most of the plants will have flowered and seeded. Hopefully, the weather will be dry and settled. We were lucky last year, our meadow hay was all cut, baled and carted inside four days. The grass will make new growth during late summer, and sheep will graze the meadows in the autumn.

July 2006

Boyhood Tales

The Great Ouse river rises just to the north-west of our district, with a coming together of two little streams from south Northamptonshire. It meanders through the pleasant meadows of our parishes and soon becomes an important feature of the local landscape, its banks hosting a diverse variety of flora and fauna. To some of us, the river is like an old friend. I have lived near it all my life; my father taught me to swim in a deep pool known as Clay Bottom. In those days, this stretch was fringed by tall willows, and a three-arch railway bridge, built of blue bricks, towered nearby. On a summer's evening after a day's haymaking or harvesting, ten or a dozen people including a family or two would gather there to swim and generally have fun. Some would run and jump straight in, while others would climb down the wooden steps, improvised from an old threshing ladder.

One summer, my friend and I made a raft from two forty-gallon barrels lashed to a timber frame; an inner tube from a tractor rear tyre was wedged under the centre for extra buoyancy. This provided lots of fun for a group of us village children – we punted along under arches of overhanging trees on some imaginative and hazardous voyages. Many days in childhood and adolescence were spent by the river. Sometimes we built dams to create deeper water for fishing or swimming; on other days we might fish for minnows and sticklebacks, leaning over the bridges with our jam jars on long strings, or catch crayfish on squares of wire netting with old pieces of meat tied on for bait. The squares would be lowered into the water on lengths of baler twine and carefully submerged under a bank for an hour or two; the meat lured the crayfish on to the netting, but they could not get off again.

Many of the old willows along the banks were felled when the river was extensively dredged in 1976, the year of the famous drought. As the excavator emptied each bucketful of sludge from the riverbed all sorts of creatures emerged. In one place about fifty eels wriggled out as we watched in surprise. I managed to catch eight or ten before they got away, and I put them in a bucket of water which I then carried home to show my father. I put the bucket down in the porch, but by the time I had fetched him they had all disappeared – slithered back to the river, no doubt. We witness the changes in the river from season to season. In droughty summers it is no more than a little brook, gently babbling peacefully over its stony bed, the deeper pools almost motionless, choked with waterweed and bulrushes. In one place nearby, yellow water lilies flower each June and July in a still, deep stretch downstream of an old railway bridge. After days of heavy winter rainfall the river becomes a raging torrent, the coffee-coloured waters eddying and whisking round trees and fence posts in their fury as extensive flooding takes place. At such times the floodwater becomes quite menacing, deserving the utmost respect. Only once have I seen the river completely frozen over, and that was in 1963 when thick ice covered the surface for several weeks; I have memories of us skating after school, by moonlight.

From Brackley to Buckingham the river threads its course either side of the disused railway branch line. The river and the railway intersect each other in several places as they pass through the parishes of Evenley, Westbury, Finmere, Water Stratford, Tingewick and Radclive. Near to Westbury the branch line passes under what was once the Great Central main line from London to Manchester, through a large steel bridge, now rusting away. When I was a boy the grass on the line banks was regularly cut short by hand by men using fagging hooks. This maintenance was an essential precaution against fire; it was quite common, especially in summer, for hot coals to fall from a passing engine and set light to the dry grass. The only other vegetation allowed to grow beside the railway was the produce of a small steep garden on a section of bank at Bacon's Crossing, tended by the crossing keeper, Mr Faulkner. The Banbury to Verney Junction branch line, to use its proper title, was twenty-one miles long and opened on May 1st 1850. In 1956, during the last decade of its one hundred and fourteen year history, a diesel rail-car service was introduced which operated between Banbury and Buckingham for a period of about four years; halts were specially constructed at Radclive and Water Stratford.

I well remember travelling from Water Stratford to Banbury; the journey only took twenty minutes in spite of several stops along the way, and the price of a ticket was 2/3d (11p). Thanks to Dr Beeching, all passenger services came to an end in 1960. The only trains to use the line after that were goods trains, and then in December 1964 the line was closed altogether. I was invited, along with my brother, sisters and a few other village children, to ride on the footplate of one of the last goods steam trains ever to pass along the line. After the line had been closed, it was used for the storage of hundreds of redundant carriages waiting to be scrapped. Rails and sleepers were eventually lifted in 1967, the trackbed was removed soon after, and finally some of the beautiful arched bridges spanning road and river were demolished. The disused railway line has now become a wonderful nature reserve. For the last thirty-five years natural regeneration has taken place largely unhindered. It is quite amazing to see how nature has reclaimed the banks and cuttings of the old line: the forest of trees and plants is impenetrable in places. There are oak, ash and sycamore trees of up to fifty feet tall, and smaller trees of hazel, crab apple and thorn. A rich mixture of wild plants thrive, providing an ideal habitat for deer, badgers, foxes, rabbits and squirrels, and a variety of birds. In fact there is today a pastoral tranquillity of the kind that might have existed up until 1847, when the navvies arrived and shattered the peace.

The river, the railway and the farm all provided opportunities for adventure for us village children. When not at school we would spend many hours outdoors, off on our bikes or walking in the fields or along the riverbank. As a boy I was always keen to go out on the farm after school. I'm afraid I regarded attendance at school as an annoying interruption to farming! Sitting in my bedroom struggling with homework on a summer's evening was particularly hard when I could hear the shearing machine clattering away over the garden fence in the field by our house, or see from my window tractors and trailers going through the village, bringing loads of silage or hay back to the farmyard. One of my classmates from up the road would sometimes join me as I hurried off 'down the farm' after school to find my father and uncles – I was anxious to see what was going on. The haymaking season was usually over before the school summer holidays began; I always thought this was so unfair. But we tried to involve ourselves with the activities of making hay whenever we could; after all, this was a great time of year to be outside, and haymaking provided opportunities for having fun and learning new skills at the same time. We were especially keen on driving the tractors that pulled the hay trailers slowly round the field, while the men loaded the bales by pitchfork. When the trailer was full we were often allowed to ride home on top of the load, provided we lay down out of sight and kept quiet.

One hot afternoon in June, the school bus dropped us off as usual. We rushed our tea, changed into old clothes and ran to find out where the men were carting hay bales from. Radclive, was the answer, and the shortest route was by way of the railway line. We crossed one field, waded through the river and jogged uphill to the railway, and started walking. Half way along the line we came across two bicycles propped up against a post. The temptation was overwhelming, so we 'borrowed' the bikes to quicken the journey, but cycling over the stone trackbed was not easy. Quite soon we passed two men working near a railwayman's hut – the owners of the bikes! They gave chase – we soon ditched the bikes and ran – all the way to the bottom of the hayfield. We lay exhausted, hiding in the long grass for a few minutes. When it was safe to do so, we climbed the hill to the top of the field, only to see in the distance the last load of hay being driven out of the gateway and on to the main road. We were just too late. It was a long and miserable dawdle home; we dared not return along the railway line.

A compilation of excerpts from 2003 and 2004

Haymaking

After school in summer,
  My friend and I would be gone
Down the lane to the hayfields,
  To work with the men on the farm;
      Flowering grasses and clover sweet,
      Ancient meadows into swaths laid neat,
      Fragrant in the balmy heat
  Of the longest days in June.

With the tractor and the swath-turner
  We were keen to make a show,
The men would tease and there would be
  Much banter, to and fro;
      But skilled young drivers we would make
      As we learned to use the old horse-rake
      And tedder, the hay to toss and shake,
  Cascading down each row.

Two swaths into one were raked
  When the hay was fit to bale;
Grass seed flew as the baler clunked,
  Behind, the sledge would trail.
      Tractors and trailers together were hitched,
      And to the field by the men were fetched,
      We boys would drive as the bales were pitched,
  Each taking turns at the wheel.

Back to the rickyard we would ride
  On a wagon-load of hay,
Passing under the tall trees
  As on our backs we lay,
      Enjoying our high escapade
      In sparkling sun and dappled shade
      With our ginger beer and lemonade
  Telling tales along the way.

Many years have passed since my friend and I
  Helped with making hay,
What became of him I do not know,
  Or where he is today;
      But bound together by a chain
      Of boyhood memories we remain,
      Brought back to me from down the lane,
  On summer's sweet bouquet.

Cheap Wheat

The steep rise in licence duty for four wheel drive vehicles is yet another blow to the countryside imposed by an urban-minded government. This 'blunt instrument' approach discriminates against those of us who run four wheel drives as essential tools of our rural businesses. These vehicles are standard equipment for farmers, and are needed for travelling across land in all weathers to tend cattle and sheep, service machinery, mend fences and countless other jobs, as well as being able to safely tow trailers carrying livestock and farm goods. Other users, for whom a four wheel drive vehicle is a necessity and not the luxury it is often perceived to be, include the police and emergency services, vets, gas, electricity and water companies, tree surgeons, forestry workers and anyone who has a need for a sturdy and reliable means of off-road transport across any type of terrain in all weathers. There must have been countless instances recently of four wheel drives coming to the aid of flood victims; my vehicle was certainly appreciated on July 21st when I drove through floodwater and over the river bridge at Fulwell to rescue someone stuck on the other side.

The torrential rain of July 20th revealed a leak in one of our roofs. Some items stored in a cupboard beneath were in danger, so I rescued them and in doing so discovered some old magazines dating from 1974, including several copies of Farmers Weekly, Country Life and a Thomson Winter Sun brochure. They make interesting reading. The price of wheat in March of that year was £68 per tonne, exactly the same price that I sold some of my wheat for last year, 2006. The early 1970s were a time of high inflation, and cereal values had doubled in less than two years. Wheat prices have fluctuated in the thirty-three years since, reaching a peak in the mid 1980s, when I sold some for £140 per tonne. Currently, the price is about £115, and the bakeries have just announced that bread will soon cost 40% more, as a result of the 'high' cost of wheat! In the winter of 1973/4, one could have flown off to the Algarve on a Thomson package deal, spending seven nights in a four star hotel for £42 per person, much less than the cost of a tonne of wheat. A similar holiday now would cost about £460, or four tonnes. Country Life reported that a new Honda Civic (three door hatchback) cost £1,159 in 1974, and a four bedroomed detached house with large garden in open country, between Winslow and Aylesbury, was for sale at £25,250. It is probably worth thirty times as much today.

The recent increase in the value of wheat has been driven by a fall in world stocks at a time of rising demand. Estimates of future supplies are being adjusted downwards, mostly because of poor weather conditions across the world's grain growing regions. Whilst some of the crops in the UK and parts of Western Europe have recently been flooded, Central and Eastern Europe have suffered unusually high temperatures with drought, resulting in yield loss. Production was down in Australia last harvest, and significant amounts of grain produced both in the USA and South America are being diverted into biofuel production. The implications of war in the Middle East and the issues arising from the instability of that region have encouraged America to invest heavily in biofuel plants in her desire for greater fuel security. This will mean that less US grain will be available on world markets in future. At the same time, China and India are consuming more grain each year, and are likely to continue to do so. In spite of all this, wheat is trading at less than it was twenty years ago, and is still cheap in real terms, being worth much less than its 1974 value.

July 2007

Yellow Peril

Old country sayings regarding the weather and the seasons are fascinating, but they cannot always be relied upon. 'Two moons in May – no harvest and no hay!' This seems to proclaim a stark warning of either very poor yields, or dreadful summer weather, or perhaps a combination of both. Despite new moons occurring on both the 1st and 31st May we have had one of the best haymaking seasons in living memory, with heavy crops of good quality hay. Harvest is also progressing well at the time of writing, greatly assisted by record breaking hot weather, following a fine St. Swithin's on July 15th. The yields, however, are not breaking any records, but at least crop prices have improved a little on the very low values of last harvest.

The midsummer wild flowers growing along our local roadsides in July and August have been delightful. Between Finmere and Westbury and across to Shalstone the verges were dotted with the purples and blues of scabious, knapweed, meadow cranesbill and tufted vetch, interspersed with pink shades of willowherb, mallow and foxglove. Dainty white flowers of yarrow and fool's parsley presented themselves along the banks either side of the lane at Fulwell, and in certain places, ladies bedstraw, which has clusters of tiny yellow flowers, and common meliot, a legume with a smell like new mown hay and also yellow flowered, could be seen on the roadsides from Wood Green to Shalstone and from Water Stratford to Finmere. Many of these plants thrive on dry limestone soils.

Not all wild flowers are desirable: common ragwort, for example, is harmful to livestock. Until about three years ago, I would have had difficulty in correctly identifying this weed, and I suspect many others would have had the same problem; you simply never saw it growing, anywhere. The recent rapid spread of ragwort has been nothing short of explosive. It can be seen locally on the roadside from Tingewick to Buckingham, along the Tingewick bypass and next to the roundabout at Finmere. It seems to have colonised the margins of motorways, landfill sites, lakes, quarries, military establishments and building sites up and down the country. In fact ragwort will grow on almost any land which remains uncultivated for a short period of time. Worryingly, I recently discovered a few plants growing in amongst some young trees in one of my new spinneys. The realisation that we had ragwort growing on the farm was upsetting. The plants were dug up and burned, but unfortunately, they had already started to shed seed. Ragwort, when eaten by animals, causes irreparable liver damage, both when it is growing in the field, and in hay or silage where it is even more dangerous because it is more palatable. Sheep are less susceptible than horses however, and most wild animals instinctively avoid the plant. Ragwort looks innocent enough with its tall stems and small daisy-like yellow flowers, but it spreads quickly because each flower produces up to 150,000 seeds. Farmers and landowners have known this for centuries, and have sought to keep land free from infestation by cutting and burning or pulling up the plants by the roots. Until the last few years, cases of ragwort poisoning have been rare, but now the menace of this harmful weed has returned, and it is not difficult to see why.

After the Second World War, the need to address problems caused by ragwort was recognised by the government. The Weed Act of 1959 gave local authorities all the power they needed to control this pernicious weed, by giving them the means to serve notice on landowners to prevent its spread, backed up by prosecution if necessary. As a result, the country remained virtually free from ragwort for fifty years. But more recently, local government has failed to use its powers to prevent infestation. I have no doubt that this is because ragwort has been allowed to spread freely over land belonging to the Highways department, and across land held by other government bodies. So the main offenders have been the government and the local authorities themselves.

August 2003

Trepidation and Exposure

The onset of harvest is both an exciting and a nerve-racking time; every cereal farmer eagerly awaits the results of the past year's work, and looks forward to the thrill of seeing the first of his grain coming off the combine. He asks himself endless questions: did I plant the right varieties? Did I use the correct amount of fertiliser? Was it applied at the right time? Perhaps I should have used more fungicide. What will the yields be like? Should I have sold some of the crop forward, or should I wait for the market to improve? Is my machinery fully prepared, and are my drying facilities adequate in case of a wet harvest? All this mounting anxiety occurs every year, and is part of the whole experience of harvest. Without it there would be no cosy feeling of satisfied relief when all is finally gathered in, safely dried and stored in the barn. The whole process of growing a crop is one long gamble from beginning to end, and the final outcome depends on many things. Top of that list is the weather, which constantly influences the development of the crop from the day it is planted to the day it is harvested. In 2007, the spring drought lowered yields, but this year the growing season has been much kinder, and potentially, there is a big wheat crop out there. The only problem is that so far we have had precious little opportunity to gather it in because of the unseasonal rains.

Combines all over the country have been standing idle throughout much of August when they should have been cutting wheat – there are about five million acres to tackle. Nowadays the workforce in agriculture is smaller than ever. In the words of St Luke's Gospel, "The harvest is plenteous, but the labourers are few." That is certainly true today, when one man plus seasonal staff often has to cope with a thousand acres or more. Such situations are quite common and normally easily achievable, provided one has the aid of reasonably up-to-date machinery and equipment – and hopefully, a little help from the weather.

Between planting time and harvest the growing corn provides plenty of cover for wild creatures who would otherwise fall prey to foxes, stoats and kestrels in far greater numbers than they already do. Kestrels don't bother to search for food above the corn once it grows tall; field mice, voles and shrews are quite safe until after harvest. Birds of prey don't like diving into the crop; the straw buckles under them, thus impeding their split second swoop, and hampering their ascending flight. Stoats and weasels are also reluctant to hunt in the base of a maturing crop of corn; the rustling sounds of the stalks and ears are confusing to them. Many small mammals and insects can live in safety until the day the combine comes. When it does, it suddenly changes their habitat beyond recognition with a cacophony of noise and dust. The next few hours provide rich pickings for the birds, as bewildered insects and field mice are exposed to the world. After the sun has gone down, owls will start to quarter the freshly cut stubble. Small mammals can no longer move about the fields in daylight, it is too dangerous. But they will soon adapt to their changed surroundings. They have to return to their nocturnal habits, and live their lives as they did before the corn grew tall.

August 2008

Another Long Day

After a shaky start, this year's harvest was eventually completed and land work is now back on schedule as we prepare for the planting of next year's crops. This is perhaps surprising when you consider that we had cut less than a quarter of our harvest by the end of August. For most of the month we were regularly subjected to tropical-style rain storms; all too often the epicentre of these 'power showers' seemed to be over our farm, and I began to feel victimised. On several occasions we took advantage of a window of dry weather and snatched a few more acres of wheat, only to be rained off again after a couple of hours. Eventually, thank goodness, the weather changed with the moon, as it often does. The full moon of August 30th brought fine weather and a rising barometer, and, at last, an opportunity to crack on. In spite of all the previous delays and difficulties, nothing could quell the excitement and enthusiasm that came with the knowledge that settled weather lay ahead, and the old harvest magic returned with the sunshine.

September 2nd was one of our best days. Tractors and trailers and the combine had all been serviced, greased and re-fuelled ready for an early start. The wheat fields we were cutting had been steam-rollered flat in places by the recent storms, and some of the crop could only be cut one-way. However, after the dew had evaporated the straw became dry and crisp, and progress was good. The day was hot and sunny and from the combine cab I could see beauty all around: the patterns in the stubble of the cut crop, the spider's webs in the standing corn, and the dust cloud from the combine constantly drifting up and away like smoke. Harvesting wheat, the king of crops, can be very satisfying, even though your adrenalin is constantly running. We did not stop at lunchtime, but ate our sandwiches on the move; I was determined to cut all the fields in this block in one session. By evening, the dust was hanging in strands across the valley, pierced by near-horizontal rays of the setting sun. The moon, still very full, rose dramatically huge and pink from behind the trees. After dark, one sees much in the way of wildlife in the work lights of the combine. At one point, as I drove to the parked trailer on the headland to empty the tank, I saw a tawny owl perched on the top of the trailer, peering out, no doubt confused by the lights.

Eventually, I finished the last field in the block of land we were cutting. I parked up the combine, wiped the dust from the cab windows and drove the final trailer-load back to the farm. Just two of us had managed to clear well over two hundred tonnes of wheat in about thirteen hours. My grandfather would have been impressed. And at last, the grain had been coming into the barn at less than fifteen per cent moisture content, so, thankfully, did not need to be dried. I switched off the lights in the grain store and rolled down the doors. I stepped outside and gazed up at the stars; the night was beautifully clear. Five or six airliners were passing silently overhead, and for a moment, I wondered about the people in those planes, and I hoped they were happy in their world, six miles up in the sky. Here on the ground I was happy with mine as I walked over to the house, tired and dusty, but with a lighter heart than of late, and with that feeling of satisfaction one gets after having completed a productive day's work. It was just after midnight and I was ready for my supper. My ears were still ringing from the noise of the harvest, but the quietness was blissful. Peace. Well, not quite… I could just faintly hear my neighbour's combine, two parishes distant, still howling away into the night.

September 2004

Cruising

She cuts across a rolling ocean,
Sailing in a stately motion.
Gracefully, she glides supreme,
In her wake a golden stream.
She cruises through the broad expanse
Beneath a solar radiance.
The headland deeps are hers to claim,
She turns, and so reveals her name:
'New Holland', high upon her side,
Her yellow paintwork shines with pride.
She sails a sea of Avalon
On a blue-gold August afternoon.
Amid the roar, the dust, the heat,
Her tank is filling up with wheat;
And she is the undisputed queen
Of this classic harvest scene.

Note: Avalon was a popular variety of wheat,
widely grown in the early 1980s.

Autumn

A Miserable Walk

It is the morning of September 10th, and the trees are still dripping after overnight rain as I set off on a walk round the farm. My intention is to assess the impact of all the recent wet weather. The water from one inch of rainfall over one acre weighs one hundred tonnes; our farm, therefore, has taken a quarter of a million tonnes of water in the last ten days. This would not be unremarkable during late autumn, winter or early spring, but coming as it has in the middle of what was already a delayed harvest, on what was already wet land, is disastrous. We were three quarters of the way through our wheat harvest when things came to an abrupt halt at 1.30am on the morning of August 31st. Fog had descended at midnight, and rain set in an hour later. A wheel has not been turned since then, and today's forecast offers no hope of fine weather in the near future. We have at least now caught up with a huge backlog of grain drying, and used an enormous amount of expensive fuel in the process.

I squelch through standing water in a gateway and down the grassy track which runs along the edge of a small wood. There are some large old ash trees here, approaching the end of their lives. Today their trunks have turned almost black, the bark soaked through with all the recent rain. Near the bottom of the wood is a small piece of land which has been the site of muckheaps in recent years. I'm sure this place is where a rickyard once was. The clues are all around in the interesting variety of wild plants that grow here, providing something of the character of all the fields on the farm. Countless harvests of the past have brought seeds from the fields to the rickyard; weeds and wild flowers gathered in on wagon loads of hay and sheaves of corn.

I walk over a culvert which carries a stream under the track. The stream bed is normally dry at this time of year, but today water is gurgling and swirling noisily under my feet. Further along the track the chirping of a cricket seems odd, out of place on this cool dreary morning. A few mallow plants are flowering next to the hedge, providing colourful spots of pink against an otherwise drab background. I turn off the track and up the hill across a field of wheat stubble. Water is lying in the ruts made by the combine. Thankfully the straw was baled and carted from these fields before the weather closed in. I reach the far side of the hill and remember that here was the place, a fortnight ago, where a young vixen, asleep in the standing wheat and invisible from the combine cab, became caught in the header and was badly injured. A mad dash followed to fetch a shotgun and dispatch the poor creature. I felt so sorry; she was very beautiful. Foxes evoke feelings like no other animal – loved and hated, respected and reviled in equal measure. I was on the side of the fox that day.

Eventually I arrive at some unharvested wheat fields. The crops are still standing, but they are looking very weathered. I rub out the grain from a soggy ear. It is as I feared – the corn is starting to sprout – little green shoots are growing out of almost every grain of wheat. These crops, if we ever harvest them, will be of very low quality. Heavy machinery on waterlogged land will cause untold damage to the soil, and long delays to seedbed preparation are now inevitable, all of which means that the planting of next year's crops is in serious jeopardy. I make my way back towards home, crossing the highest part of the farm. Normally I would linger here – I love the view; but drizzle is falling now and visibility is poor. I hurry back to the house and computer to check the weather forecast for the umpteenth time in the last few days.

September 2008

Sharing Garden Produce

This has been a bumper year for plums. The first fruit from our plum trees came at the end of July, from a young, heavily laden tree planted seven years ago, which I think is an Opal. These early blue plums are small and sweet, and they ripen surprisingly quickly. One day we noticed one or two had already fallen; I knew they should have been picked without delay, but we were too busy at the time. The following morning we found the lower branches had been broken down and stripped of fruit, and the surrounding grass had been trampled. Deer, most likely muntjac, had paid a nocturnal visit. The remaining plums were quickly infested with wasps, so we lost most of the fruit from that tree. Next to ripen were plums from a Victoria, which were also spoiled by wasps, and by the third week of August greengages and goldengages were almost ready, from trees also only a few years old. Several nights earlier, we had been woken by a muntjac barking in the garden, so I was expecting further damage. Knowing how even a dim light burning at night will keep a fox away from a henhouse, I placed some solar powered garden lights at the foot of the trees, hoping for the same result. It seemed to work – there has been no sign of the deer since, and we have very much enjoyed our first decent crop of gages.

At the beginning of September our yellow plums were ready. I don't know the variety except that it is an old-fashioned one, but these large, golden plums are delicious. The trees were given to us by my late uncle, soon after we moved here eleven years ago. He could not have given us a more thoughtful gift – they are easy to grow, coming true from suckers, which he originally dug up from his own farmhouse garden. They seem to be fairly resistant to pests and disease, and are high yielding; I've never seen so much fruit on them as we have had this year. To be able to pick and eat fruit straight from the garden is a pleasure, and the flavour of plums embodies, for me, the very essence of summer's completeness – the taste of the season itself, mysteriously created in the precious weeks from blossom to maturity.

A couple of weeks later we started picking our cobnuts; they were not really quite ready, but we were determined to beat the squirrels this year – they will take the lot if allowed to. The same applies to the walnuts, although these are still too green to pick at present. If some of the produce from the garden has to be shared with the local wildlife, so be it. One just has to remember to plant enough for them in the first place. Unsurprisingly, no wild creature has ever been interested in our medlars, and we don't know what to do with them either. The strange, unattractive fruits are hard and intensely bitter, and the skin becomes wrinkled with age. I am told that they should be harvested in November, after a few frosts, and stored until they become soft. Somehow we always seem to forget about them.

We watched a beautiful sunset last night, which seemed to announce the beginning of autumn. The tall poplars down by the stream are already losing their leaves; they always fall from the lower branches first, and will finally disappear from the tops in a few weeks time. By the end of November, they will be bare. The wind has whispered in these trees all summer long, and even when there seems to be no discernible current of air, the leaves are always moving. Each summer, I become used to the comforting sighing one hears when standing nearby, reminiscent of the rippling waters of a shallow brook, running over pebbles. When winter comes, the wind will blow through the naked branches, making a different sound altogether.

September 2009

Irrepressible Nature

Very little garden watering was necessary during the wet summer, and the lawns have remained a vibrant shade of green usually seen only in spring. The rain has been good for the trees, but our field hedges, which seem to have made twice their normal growth this year, are in need of attention. Waterlogged ground did not allow access for the hedge cutter last winter, and our hedges are now overgrown and festooned with unruly brambles and briar. It will be quite a task to trim them back into shape, and the difficulty is timing. Waiting until the birds have eaten all the berries is preferable, but the land may be too wet to travel on by then. We used to rely on hard weather during winter for this job, but frost is no longer guaranteed. If hedges have not been cut by the end of February, they will have to wait for yet another year because by then the birds will be nesting again.

It is amazing how quickly nature will take over when man's regular intervention is suspended. There is a good example of this in a field near the top of the farm, where a spring used to supply the village with water via an underground pipe, before mains was connected about eighty years ago. A bog developed in part of the field after the water had been diverted, which made growing a crop on this small area impossible. Attempts to drain the spring to a nearby ditch have been many and various over the years, and mostly have not lasted long because of running sand in the subsoil. Exceptionally, in 1975 we were able to grow potatoes there, followed by a successful crop of forage maize in 1976, but after these two dry years the area quickly reverted to bog. A couple of years later we were cleaning ditches, and whilst we had a digger on the farm, I took the opportunity to get the driver to dig a big hole to try to reconnect drains to the spring. This partly succeeded, and the hole became a pond. I planted five oak trees nearby, and mowed the surrounding area for a couple of years afterwards. It was then mostly neglected; brambles and hawthorn became established. Only two of my planted oaks now survive, and these are poor, spindly specimens, but they are surrounded by many larger healthy trees of oak and ash which have grown since, coming naturally from seeds dispersed by wind, proving that nature prefers to control its own destiny.

Seeds can lie dormant for a long time in some unlikely places. Many years ago the river was dredged and some of the spoil was spread on low-lying places in the adjacent meadow. A few weeks later these patches were yellow with the flowers of thousands of tall kale plants – this was a complete mystery to me until my father explained that during the war, the meadow was ploughed up by order of the War Office to grow kale for seed production. Some of the seeds that shed must have blown into the water, becoming buried in the river bed for nearly forty years, but they remained viable and capable of germinating when the right conditions presented themselves. The environment, and especially the soil, is full of seeds just waiting for a chance to grow.

In the autumn of 2003 I decided to convert a small strip of former set-aside land next to the garden to an area of grass and trees where, once suitable species had been established, I would try to introduce some wild flowers. The heavy clay soil was very dry that season, and my grass seed mixture was slow to establish. After two years of regular mowing, digging out thistles and docks and re-planting bare patches, I was disappointed with the result, being reminded of why I had set the land aside in the first place. Last year I decided not to mow until July, thereby creating an opportunity for seed to shed. This allowed yellow hawkbit and buttercup to flower, providing colour and food for butterflies and bees. I repeated the same regime this year, and we were surprised and delighted to discover bee orchids flowering in June. Few of the plants growing there now were sown by me; most have come from the vast reserves of seed already contained within the soil.

September 2007

Harvest Home

As the last few days of this glorious summer slip away, the seasonal changes are becoming apparent. But autumn proper is still a way off yet, and just now we seem to be in a kind of extra season, in between summer and autumn. The sun is still very warm on these calm dry days; the evenings are balmy, and working outside continues to be a pleasure. The trees and hedges are as green as ever, but there is something almost indefinable about the quality of the light, the behaviour of the birds, the smell of the air even; something that seems to be warning us that these days will not last. Harvest has come and gone and we have arrived at the end of another farming year, and at the same time, the start of a new one. Most calendars begin on January 1st and end on December 31st; they are usually produced in bright colours on glossy paper with attractive pictures, but to read the farming calendar you must study the fields. They are imprinted with the effects of sun, wind, rain and frost according to the seasonal variations brought about by constantly changing levels of light and length of days, all of which control growth. The farmer must live by the farming calendar, which begins and ends on Michaelmas Day, September 29th.

Life on the farm has been increasingly busy since the spring, with spreading and spraying, drilling, shearing, silage and haymaking, right through to the corn harvest, which began with winter barley and ended with linseed. Oilseed rape, oats, peas, wheat and beans all came in between. As soon as one crop was cleared, the next was ripe and ready for the combine. The straw had to be dealt with too; baling and carting was organised in turn. Harvest may now be over, but farmers cannot relax: time is short and cultivations must begin as soon as the straw has been cleared – the soil needs time to weather before seedbeds can be created in preparation for the sowing of next year's crops. As autumn unfolds, the landscape will go through its seasonal changes like a film in ultra slow motion, gradually revealing fresh colours which, since early summer, will have gone from pale shades of green to cream, gold and bronze, then brown and hopefully back to green as the miracle of growth starts all over again, ensuring that we shall have another harvest, just as we are giving thanks for this one.

Before long the fields will be strangely quiet again, and memories of the noise and haste of the last few weeks will diminish. Only when autumn planting has been completed can farmers slow down a little and enjoy the satisfaction of knowing that 'all is safely gathered in', a pleasant state of mind as old as farming itself. Life was so much simpler for those working the land in bygone days, they had no forms to fill in, and no worries about the relationship between the pound and the euro, or the price of fertiliser. But they had their own problems. Their concern was simply whether the harvest had been good enough to allow them to feed their families and their animals over the coming winter. We are lucky to live in a land of plenty; the production of our crops today is greatly assisted by modern technology – our harvests hardly ever fail completely. Some of our worst bugbears are caused not so much by pests or diseases (we can control most of them) but by bureaucracy.

Every harvest has its memories, good and bad, but already I have almost forgotten my frustration when the combine lost power in a wheat crop because of a fuel problem, and when, two weeks later, the linseed would not cut and became wrapped around the auger and the reel. But I have happy memories of ten golden days in August when the combine swept back and forth over the wheat fields and the barn filled steadily with dry grain. It is good that we still celebrate Harvest Home with our village harvest suppers, when the whole community shares in the feeling of good-humoured satisfaction and gratitude that all the crops in the parish have been harvested and are safely stored for another year – a sensation just as relevant and in keeping with the season as it ever was. The harvest suppers of the past would have had a romance all of their own I imagine, much like the one described in Hardy's 'Far from the Madding Crowd', when most of the men in the parish worked on the land. They all sat down with their families to a feast in the Great Barn, celebrating the culmination of the year's work. Nowadays, we farmers employ hydraulics, electronic monitoring systems and computer technology in our machinery, and we communicate by e-mail and mobile phone. The thatched ricks of hay and horse-drawn wagon-loads of sheaves are long gone, but when harvest is over, we still experience the same feelings of relief and contentment as those who worked the land before us.

September 2003

Gratitude

Harvest came early; pressure was high;
Long days working in the heat passed by
In a swirling, dusty cloud.
These fields were ploughed
Some time ago;
Dry soil came up
In lumps as big as horses' heads,
Early morning gossamer hung for weeks
In flimsy threads across the furrows.

The land lay waiting
Under baking skies of August and September,
As dry a time as ever I remember,
Waiting for rain to soften the clay
That it might be fit another day
To take the seeds of next year's harvest.
We scanned horizons near and farthest
For any hopeful signs of rain;
The glass could not fall back until
Another moon should wax and wane.

Seed wheat, cleaned, dressed and bagged
Lay ready in the barn for planting,
Belying the rock-hard clods;
Late summer sunshine left us wanting.
Birdsong had diminished
Save for the monotony of pigeons calling
Tediously, and without passion.
A hungry garden blackbird
Pecked in desultory fashion
Across the dry, cracked lawn,
And in amongst the flower beds;
His manner quite forlorn.
One day, in haste,
He followed me to the compost heap,
And for the opportunity
To search the kitchen waste
For a few meagre scraps
Was grateful, perhaps.

Yesterday, it started raining,
Steady rain, all night.
And this morning
The rain is still falling, gentle and light.
The birds are all singing in the rain,
Trying to out-do each other,
As though it were spring again.
But now it's Michaelmas!
And, at this time of thankfulness
For harvest, my spirit soared,
For I heard that blackbird singing out
Above all other birds,
And I knew why.
We shared an impulse of gratitude,
The blackbird and I.

The sun came out; wet grass glistened;
The blackbird sang so beautifully!
I listened
To his melodic notes of purest fluting clarity,
Declaring from a treetop
That he no longer needs my charity;
Singing out to celebrate the rain,
Which for him, falls for no other reason
Than to bring tasty earthworms to the surface.
But all good things, in their proper season,
Ultimately depend on rain;
For me and the blackbird it surely does allow
Abundance: he will not go hungry now.
But nonetheless it will be strange,
After all these arid weeks,
To tread soft soil again
And see the water-butt filled.
The blackbird enjoyed his first autumn feast,
And now the wheat can be drilled.

Ploughmen and Showmen

All the growth of spring and summer had reached its natural fulfilment by harvest time, the season that I think of as being the climax of the year. Harvest ended on this farm in early September, and with it, the last of the summer weather. Michaelmas approaches as the swallows gather on the wires, and now we must acknowledge the onset of autumn. The days are still mellow, but there is a sense of decline as the year starts to wind down; this is the bitter-sweet prelude to the harsh winter months ahead, and worst of all, the darkness. In a few weeks the appearance of the landscape will have changed completely: many fields will be green with newly planted crops while others may have been ploughed and left to 'weather' over the coming months, ready for sowing in the spring. Some land will remain in stubble, going grey as time passes by, while leys and pastures change to paler greens as the temperature drops and the grass stops growing.

This autumn we are direct drilling most of our winter wheat into the stubbles of the previous crops of peas, beans and oilseed rape in order to save fuel, but it has been necessary to plough some fields in the traditional way. Ploughing has been carried out since man first tilled the earth, and although the modern tractor and plough is light years ahead of the oxen and crude wooden implements of ancient times, the process itself remains essentially the same. The soil is sliced through and turned over to bury weeds and previous crop residues, whilst any compaction is relieved and drainage is improved. At the same time a fresh surface of soil is exposed which can be worked into a seedbed in preparation for the next crop. Ploughing is a very satisfying job – you never tire of looking back over your shoulder from the tractor seat to see your plough turning the soil; the furrows rise in waves and settle back in neat rows as the old stubble constantly disappears under the mouldboards. The intoxicating scent of fertility rises from the freshly turned earth, carrying with it the promise of renewal. The act of ploughing is like drawing a line under all that has gone before; it marks the start of a new beginning: the slate is wiped clean. The skill and concentration of the tractor driver is rewarded by the creation of straight and even furrows; the appearance of his work is a matter of pride as well as being important for reasons of good husbandry. Neat and level ploughing with all trash buried is aesthetically pleasing; the field is the canvas on which the ploughman becomes the artist, but he has no control over who sees the results. The furrows might not be visible for long however; the land may soon be levelled by subsequent cultivation and the action of the seed drill. Ideally, and weather permitting of course, winter wheat should be sown by the first Saturday of Buckingham Fair.

The origins of our local fair can be traced back to an ancient Royal Charter, granted to the town of Buckingham in 1554 by Mary Tudor. Charters were devised as a means of regulating fairs and markets, in effect giving permission for them to be held on certain dates of the year, in return for which revenue would be paid to the Crown. For hundreds of years fairs all over the country have been centres of trade and amusement. Hiring fairs, or mop fairs as they are known in the Midlands and Cotswolds, were often held on the same day as the charter fair and provided local opportunities for those seeking work in the countryside to introduce themselves to prospective employers. Since the mid 1800s however, the business which originally took place at fairgrounds has been conducted elsewhere; the sole purpose of today's fairs is to provide entertainment. C.W. Hatfield, writing in 1868, described a fair as 'An open space crowded with a dense motley assemblage of shows, booths, stalls, swings, roundabouts, wheels of fortune, shooting galleries, photographic tents, panoramas, weighing machines, hawkers, cheapjacks, beggars, ginger beer vendors, ballad singers, quacks, fiddlers, brass instrument players, policeman, thieves, unfortunates, dissolute vagabonds and other usual accompaniments at such gatherings'.

September 2005

Hot Air

When the summer heatwave ended and the weather broke in the second week of August, cereal farmers fell into two groups: those who had finished harvest and those who had not. My combine had been cleaned off ready for winter storage, after having completed our crops of wheat and beans by mid August – the earliest finish for many years. But after two weeks of unsettled weather it was back in action again in early September, when I was called upon to help a neighbour finish his harvest. A few pleasant combining days followed in the mellow late summer sunshine, but by then the crops were weather-beaten, and I had to reduce forward speed so as to be able to cope with the flattened wheat. Something I shall remember about the harvest of 2006, apart from the very hot weather, was the constant need to climb down from the combine to drag fallen branches from the uncut crop. Most places were affected by severe thunderstorms in July, and we got ours on the 22nd when over 50mm of rain fell in less than two hours; at one stage there was a river flowing through our courtyard. The accompanying wind thrashed the trees and hedges with such ferocity that many branches were twisted and torn away, and carried twenty yards or more into the fields. Attempting to clear the debris before harvest would have caused even more damage to the surrounding crops; the best way was to pull the boughs out onto the stubble at the time of cutting. We must expect more of these tropical-type storms in future, so we are told, as the climate changes.

All has long since been safely gathered in, and harvest is just a memory now, but what will happen to the crops now stored on UK farms? Wheat is Britain's biggest crop, with about fifteen million tonnes being produced annually. Of this, around two million tonnes are exported, seven million tonnes are used for animal feed and six million tonnes goes into the food processing industry for human consumption. In addition to traditional uses there has been much talk recently of crops being grown to make fuel. Growing crops for energy is nothing new. Until the First World War, almost one third of farmland was used to grow grass for grazing and hay production just to feed the horses which provided power on the land and transport on the roads. A fair proportion of oats and other crops were also used for horse feed. There is now a desperate need to reduce our consumption of fossil fuels, and to switch to more secure and sustainable energy supplies.

Modern technology allows diesel to be produced from oilseed rape, and both wheat and sugar beet are capable of producing bio-ethanol. The scientists are saying that burning fuel made from crops (biofuel) does not add to global warming, because no more CO_2 is released when burning biofuel than was locked up by the growing crops in the first place. Biofuel, therefore, is apparently 'carbon neutral'. Farmers are obliged, under the current agricultural policy imposed by Europe and administered by Defra, to set aside well over a million acres of land each year. You would think, therefore, that the government might recognise these factors as a win-win situation. Set-aside land could be used to grow biofuel crops, thus saving precious fossil fuels, whilst meeting the obligations the government has committed itself to regarding renewable energy, carbon emissions and climate change. The biofuel industries of France, Germany and other European countries are growing thanks to the support of their respective governments; meanwhile ours has hardly started. Our Chancellor has recently increased the tax on biodiesel, making it uncompetitive at the pumps in comparison with conventional diesel. Until we have the political leadership which encourages a co-ordinated and integrated approach to renewable energy, the UK will remain increasingly dependent on gas from Russia, oil from the Middle East and coal from Australia, and all the platitudes about cutting greenhouse gases will continue to be nothing more than hot air.

September 2006

Pollarding and Coppicing

A recent spell of wet weather put a stop to cultivations for a few days, and whilst waiting for things to improve we have been attending to some trees on the farm. Several willows have been pollarded, a job which was long overdue. I admit that I have been putting off tackling the willows because I like the way arching boughs overhang the stream, while others grace some of the farm's tracks, providing shade in summer with long tresses of leaf. But if willows are not managed, storms will eventually cause limbs to break, and the main trunks will crack and split, condemning the tree to a slow death. We have removed the boughs from several trees accordingly, albeit with some reluctance. I shall miss hearing the distinctive sound of the wind blowing through cascades of willow leaves next summer, but by the following summer the trees will have regained their character with new growth, and hopefully we will have prolonged their lives. A few clumps of ash were coppiced at the same time; we now have large quantities of cordwood. The willow is of no use, so a few log piles have been made on field edges which will create habitats for many kinds of bugs, creatures and fungi as decay sets in. The ash will be stacked for a year or two before it warms the house. There are three plantations of poplar on the farm, all planted between 25 and 35 years ago, when a future timber cash crop was envisaged. These trees are now mature or past maturity, but strangely there is no market for the timber. One autumn a few years back, a storm toppled some of them, and the trunks of several others were snapped off. It is not worth spending time clearing the debris, so I shall simply let nature take its course.

On a quiet October morning a fortnight ago, I drove a tractor down our lane to work in some fields at the lower end of the farm. Thin veils of mist were slowly clearing, and weak sunshine, barely strong enough to cast shadows, began to enhance the reds and golds of the maples in the little wood by the bridleway. There are several ash trees along the roadside here, and their leaves were still bright green and looking as fresh as ever. The sun grew stronger by mid morning, and the day turned out to be pleasantly warm. The air was still, and yet when I came back up the lane in the late afternoon, those same ash trees were steadily shedding their leaves, and evidently had been doing so for some hours; parts of the road were now almost covered. There had been no recent frost or strong wind, but when the time comes for ash leaves to fall, fall they must. Some hornbeams I planted a few years ago, although deciduous, are never bare. They are turning yellow now, and the leaves will be shrivelled to a burnt coffee colour in a month, but because these trees are still young, they will hold their leaves until April, and only when new buds begin to break will they finally let them go.

In spite of this year's farming difficulties, it is still a prvilige to live and work in the countryside, and to see nature's treasures on a daily basis. Autumn brings many treats, including 'Hedgerow Jelly', a preserve made by distilling the juices of whatever the hedges yield. This year it has been crab apples, elderberries, sloes and blackberries, and a few Bramley apples for good measure. Another pleasure was the full moon which occurred in mid October, happily coinciding with clear weather, giving us a few bright nights with lovely starry skies. Thank goodness we don't suffer from light pollution here, so we can still enjoy the sky at night. Walk the fields by moonlight and you experience a different world; familiar features seem strange in the unearthly gleam. Senses are sharpened, and the pale silvery light is attractive in such a rare and exciting dimension. A few clouds drift across the moon, and at once become ancient works of art as each is briefly illuminated in turn. When they have passed, a panorama of stars returns. Time taken to contemplate the heavens lends perspective to our lives, and somehow connects us with both the past and the future at the same time. Many stars no longer actually exist, but we can still see them shine; I find that quite awesome.

October 2008

A New Farming Year

I was walking the fields one bright autumn morning to check on some farming issues. First stop was our small sheep flock, recently dipped, wormed and run through the footbath, and moved the day before on to some fresh grazing. All was well; I found them lying contentedly in their new surroundings. Acre after acre of pasture was dressed in silky threads, enhanced by morning dew and early sunlight. Millions of newborn spiders, when prompted to disperse at this time of year by warm weather, climb to the tops of hedges and fences where they produce strands of gossamer. A light breeze causes them to become airborne, carrying the spiders along until they drift down on to the ground, covering the fields in a network of fine lace.

After the dry September, which brought us weather more pleasant than any we had seen in July or August, I was wondering if the rains of early October would have been in time to trigger a late flush of field mushrooms. They only grow in certain places – you have to know where to look – but finding these treasures in the grass is always exciting, especially if they are still fresh and have not been trampled by cattle or sheep, or become old and struck by fly. I was disappointed to find no sign of them on that morning; an autumn without mushrooms is unusual. However, they are very fussy and will only come if conditions are just right. Cool nights, damp misty mornings and warm sunshine are needed, but sufficient rainfall in September is vital to activate the spores which lie in the ancient turf, so that they can unlock the secrets that only old pastures know.

My next job was to inspect the recently planted wheat. In a few short weeks, these fields have been turned around from one crop to the next, as a new farming year begins. Walking over the freshly drilled land was like treading on a soft carpet, the damp, crumbly soil having the consistency of brown sugar but with the right degree of firmness so as to discourage slug activity and provide good contact between seed and soil. In hindsight, we chose the perfect time to plant our wheat. This was part luck, and part judgement. I had been tempted many times in the preceding dry and dusty weeks to try and force a seedbed using my power-harrow, but by being patient and waiting for rain before drilling, we have saved a considerable amount of diesel and metal wearing parts. In any case, Mother Nature put the final touch to our seedbeds in a way that we could never have done.

We do not know yet, of course, whether this wheat will make us any money. Last year's crop certainly did not, but the crop from the previous year did. Yields were similar for both years, but growing costs and crop values have fluctuated wildly. The prices of most of the other crops we grow are strongly influenced by the ex-farm price of wheat, so the uncertainty applies to them too. Farming has gone through a two year roller-coaster ride of economic volatility, making cash-flow forecasting and cropping decisions very difficult indeed. Future investment will be suppressed while milk and grain prices remain at or below the cost of production. The unpalatable truth is that most farm businesses could not survive without European subsidies.

Farmers are constantly being sent mixed messages. We are told that food shortages will in future become common because of climate change and increases in population, and we must therefore step up production in order to satisfy increasing demand. Meanwhile, Defra secretary Hilary Benn is proposing a "re-wilding" of the countryside. Apparently, this will involve the re-introduction of species now extinct in the UK, such as the elk, the wolf and the lynx. Bad news then, for cereals and grass, free-range poultry, sheep and lambs. Sea eagles and beavers have already been reintroduced in Scotland, with consequential threats to livestock, crops and woodland. What next, I wonder? The black rat, perhaps. Will it be followed by bears and woolly mammoths?

October 2009

A Grey Area

We are looking out from our kitchen onto the lawn on a bright October morning. Under the silver birch a grey squirrel is busy with some conkers he has collected from a nearby horse chestnut. It is fascinating to watch his endearingly jerky movements as he digs around or clasps a conker between his front paws and has brief nibble. Suddenly he darts out of sight, only to reappear a moment later, scampering along a low branch. He jumps to the ground, and scurries amongst the fallen leaves seizing another conker, which he quickly buries in the lawn. An apparently innocent, amusing and typically English wildlife scene, you may think. But all is not as it should be.

The grey squirrel is a native of the east coast of North America, and was introduced into the UK quite recently, only one hundred and thirty years ago. Most of England, Wales and lowland Scotland have become colonised, and the grey has adapted readily to our climate and countryside, where it has few predators. This foreigner has similar requirements, in terms of diet and habitat, to our native red squirrel, which has lived here since the ice age, but because the grey is nearly twice the size of the red squirrel and lives at greater population densities, competition between the two has been overwhelmingly in favour of the grey. This has caused such a disastrous decline of the red squirrel that only a few small colonies survive, mainly in parts of Wales and Cumbria; they have all but vanished from the rest of England. Two of the reasons why the dominant grey has increased at the expense of the more timid and benign red squirrel are as follows. Woodland food resources are taken first by the grey – for example, greys eat unripe hazelnuts whereas reds will only take ripe ones. So all the nuts are gone before they are ripe enough for the red squirrel. Secondly, the grey squirrel carries a virus, which poses no particular threat to them, but is deadly to the red squirrel. The apparently charming behaviour of greys is deceptive; they can be fierce fighters and have been known to attack dogs, and very rarely, humans. Their bite is severe – and once attached to a victim, they don't let go.

Personally, I have good reason to dislike grey squirrels. As I walked into a spinney of ours, one morning back in June, I saw immediately that something was wrong. I was dismayed to find long strips of bark hanging from seven young hornbeam trees that I had planted fifteen years ago.

The bark had been torn away by grey squirrels from the top of the tree down to about five feet from the ground; in each case the main trunk and some branches had been affected. Last year I had discovered similar damage to some twenty-five year old maple trees in another small wood. These trees will probably survive, but in a severely disfigured form; they will never fulfil their true potential. It has long been acknowledged that grey squirrels are extremely destructive to young woodland, and the Forestry Commission has been running research programmes on control methods for the protection of trees for many years. Studies have also sought to evaluate the threat posed by grey squirrels to the native red squirrel and other wildlife; for example, they often take the eggs and young of some woodland birds. This research has revealed that small scale localised culling of greys has been a failure. If red squirrels are ever to be successfully reintroduced and our trees preserved the grey must be forced to retreat from sites where reintroduction of the red may be possible, and this will involve culling. To those who wince at the thought of killing these apparently cute-looking creatures, it should be pointed out that culling is the only sensible way to control an aggressive, alien species. By failing to contain them we will be allowing the continued destruction of woodland and there will be no hope of ever seeing the native red squirrel back where he belongs.

October 2005

A Season for Everything

British Summer Time ends this weekend, when the clocks go back one hour. If I had my way, they would stay as they are all year round. I am familiar with the arguments concerning this subject, but the fact remains that whatever time we set our clocks to it will still be dark for over sixteen hours on December 21st and for only about six hours on June 21st. It is natural, as far as modern living allows, that we should live our lives in time with the sun and in harmony with the seasons. Among other things, this means enjoying locally produced food in its proper time, when taste and freshness are at their best; the first choice for everyone should be seasonal British produce. This is the biased view of a farmer, of course, but I'm sure our senses of the seasons are being dulled by the supermarket culture of endless choice the whole year round.

Food is available today from all over the world, presented in a bewildering display of marketing and labelling styles. Fruit and vegetables labelled 'organic' but flown in from half-way across the world makes a nonsense of supermarket claims to be 'green' – this food should be labelled 'jet-lagged' instead of 'fresh'. To many people, food labelling remains confusing. It is still not generally realised that when imported food is re-packaged in this country, retailers are allowed, in certain circumstances, to display the Union Flag on the label, thus giving the impression that the contents are of British origin. Only one in three of the apples we eat today are grown in this country. The increasing flood of cheap imports over the last twenty years has discouraged traditional apple growers from reinvesting in their orchards, and only one third of the registered fruit growers who were in business in the mid 1980s now survive, even though English apples usually taste far better than imported ones.

Previous generations appreciated the seasons, and experienced the rhythms of the year much more through their food than we do today. This was partly because more of the population was either directly involved in agriculture and farm-related industries, or had family members who were employed on the land. Gardening and cookery were taught in schools, and people grew most of their own food in their gardens and allotments before the tide of urbanisation started to spread, causing this country to become overcrowded. A good deal of former allotment land has been built on since

World War II. In those days, all meat (which was properly hung) came from neighbourhood butchers, and fruit and vegetables were either bought from the local market or greengrocer, or were home-grown. Produce was never graded for shape, uniformity or colour, or any other characteristic that supermarkets today assume their customers want. Some people are striving to return to this way of living, by using farm shops, local butchers and farmers' markets, but they are still very much in the minority. The food lobby in this country is very powerful, and sometimes it uses that power irresponsibly. A health minister has recently said that obesity is by far the biggest challenge facing the health of the nation, with 23% of the adult population being overweight, the highest figure for any country in Europe. Unhealthy diets and an increase in the consumption of junk food are partly to blame, along with supermarket 'ready' meals, microwave ovens and lack of exercise. Lack of time is another factor, with people working longer hours. In an effort to keep fit, some people will drive to the gym only to ride a bike which doesn't go anywhere!

Everyone nowadays is so well connected by the latest technology, with e-mail, mobile phones and the internet, but many have become disconnected from the land and take little notice of the changing the seasons. They have forgotten where their food comes from, assuming that 'All good gifts around us…' are sent from Tescos. Perhaps this explains why attendances at Harvest Festivals have declined. Only a few years ago, a full church was almost guaranteed. Sometimes I think we should turn the clocks back, not for one hour, but for about fifty years.

October 2006

In the Woods

The woods and hedgerows on this farm have yielded an abundance of wild fruit this autumn; elderberries, rose hips, haws and blackberries have all been plentiful, providing winter food for birds from hedges which are cut once in two or three years, instead of annually. Crab apples and sloes are still in evidence, and I have never seen so many acorns on the oaks. In the garden, crops of hazelnuts and walnuts were promising, but as usual, grey squirrels took them all long before they were ripe enough to pick. Six years ago we planted a new hedge along the boundary of a meadow, using a mixture of hazel, hawthorn, dog rose, blackthorn, field maple and crab apple. When the plants were collected from the nursery, stocks of blackthorn had run out, and we were supplied instead with cherry plum (prunus myrobalana). The hedge has developed well, and at the end of August we were surprised to find a big crop of attractive reddish-yellow fruit with a sweet taste – a welcome if unexpected bonus.

Horse chestnut, ash, walnut, willow and poplar have now lost their leaves, but generally speaking the trees and hedges have stayed greener for longer this season. I always think that ash and walnut are poor value when it comes to leaf cover, their leaves being amongst the last to appear in spring and the first to fall in autumn. One of our small areas of woodland consists mainly of young Norway and field maple, and sunshine on their seasonally-coloured leaves of reds, oranges and yellows makes a fine show just now. I like walking through this wood, slowly, quietly and without the dogs – there is a fair chance of seeing a tawny owl, silently leaving its perch in one of the larger trees on a brief flight to another tree a short distance away. It is a pleasure to witness wildlife living in natural surroundings. Most movement of wild creatures takes place in a world hidden from the eyes of man; our presence usually signals the threat of danger, causing creatures to suspend their activities until we have passed by. However, if you are prepared to be still and wait for a while in a quiet spot, patience is often rewarded with a glimpse of the comings and goings of wild things.

A few fields away there is another small wood, but this wood is very old and quite wild, the result of centuries of natural regeneration with minimal interference from man. The main trees here are ash, oak, willow, hazel and aspen, with fallen boughs and rotting remains of what once were some huge elm trees lying amongst the under-storey of tangled clumps of bramble and thorn. Ivy entwines some of the willows and smaller ash trees, and occupies much of the floor space not already taken. As I walk into the wood from an adjacent field, it is as though I have crossed a threshold and entered into an entirely different domain. After only a few paces I have left behind the modern world with all its cares and haste. With any luck, no distant rumble of traffic or hum of planes will spoil the experience. No evidence of the 21st century, or indeed of any age, exists. The tracery of the branches, shapes and colours of the leaves, the patterns of the bark on the trees, and growth habit of the plants all appear the same today as they must have done to our forefathers hundreds of years ago. As I stand and gaze up into the canopy, I could easily imagine that I have stepped back in time, or even out of time altogether; the wood is a timeless, ageless place of great peace. Today, the sun, moon and stars appear just as they did in the past, the wind blows and the rain falls. The seasons come and go in the continuous cycle of darkness and light, heat and cold, renewal and decay; the birds sing and clouds pass overhead, just as they always have done.

November 2006

Feathers and Leaves

Another year is dying, and one of the most obvious symptoms is the season's colours. One autumn a few years ago I visited the arboretum at Westonbirt in Gloucestershire, and the displays there certainly did not disappoint. I often think, however, that we are lucky to live in our own arboretum, here in the parishes of North Bucks. After all, ours is a fairly wooded landscape, and over the last few weeks we have enjoyed the colour changes that each tree and shrub has shown in turn, in its own time and natural setting. The oaks in particular have now reached their autumn zenith, and this was most apparent to me today on this early November afternoon, when I walked towards some distant oak trees with the sun behind me. The leaves were already bronzed, and the setting sun further enhanced them in a final blaze of gold before sinking below the horizon.

Ten minutes later in the fading light I was passing along a bank near those trees. I found a feather in the grass, quite distinctive, a pale sandy colour on one edge, fading to almost white on the other, with three or four dark brown bars smudged across. It was a wing feather, and unmistakably that of a barn owl. The sight of an owl, silently floating at dusk over the land like a white ghost, is one that everyone remembers. It is not difficult to see how these shy, nocturnal birds became associated with wisdom and witchcraft in the past. Today, life is far from easy for barn owls. Suitable places for shelter and sites for nesting have become rare; rustic old buildings in remote places preferred by barn owls have often been demolished or converted for modern use, and natural alternatives such as large hollow trees are also disappearing.

Owls normally feed on field mice, voles and other small mammals, but unfortunately, they are often attracted to dangerous places to hunt for their food, like busy roadside verges, where prey is plentiful. Owls hunt at night by slowly quartering an area back and forth, about ten or fifteen feet from the ground; it is hard to imagine a more hazardous place for this type of activity than next to fast-moving traffic. Car headlights often cause confusion too, with disastrous results. A few weeks ago we obtained some owl boxes, made by the inmates of the prison at Grendon Underwood. They have been fixed up in various trees on the farm, in the hope of providing shelter for living and breeding in relative safety, near to food sources. For those who are interested in seeing high quality close-up images of local birds, mammals, butterflies and other creatures, together with an impressive variety of indigenous plants, I recommend a visit to www.moorhen.me.uk. All the shots are taken in a wild 'garden' which was created in the early nineties, within twenty miles of our local area.

From a farming point of view, I shall be very pleased to draw a line under this year. By the end of October we had, albeit with some difficulty, planted our intended acreage of winter wheat, but in some fields we have made a rough job of it because the soil was in such poor condition as a result of two consecutive wet summers. To date only one of eight fields intended for spring planting has yet been ploughed. Our clay soils are now too wet to allow us to continue with this job, and will almost certainly remain so throughout the winter. Our only hope is frost, which if sharp enough for several days, may briefly allow us back on to the land. More than any other implement, the plough possesses the power to change. It transforms the land at a stroke, burying the past and creating a blank canvas; it is a powerful and positive force of hope for the future, initiating the beginning of a fresh chapter in the life of the soil. I can't wait.

November 2008

The Seeds Unsown

November sheds her tears…
The floods and droughts of ninety hopeful years
Have come and gone since they signed The Armistice.
Rain thrashes the trees
And we, in reverence, on our knees
Can hardly hear the preacher for the torrents on the roof.
I wouldn't want to be caught out in this,
Unless my coat was bulletproof

Today, the Great War seems strangely near…
Almost recent, like the harvest, just passed,
Which left us with a barn full of spoilt grain.
We were very late cutting the corn this year,
Delayed, time after time, by rain.

We stand at the memorial;
Each of us imagine
Hellish theatres of war… gas, bullets, shells and blood;
We lay wreaths.
These last few days the fields have turned to mud.
The wind has blasted off the leaves,
And water lying everywhere cuts short the possibility
Of planting autumn seeds.

We give thanks for our daily bread,
And acknowledge the futility of that war;
Knowing that not a single drop of all the blood which was shed
Did, to the world, an end to conflict bring,
Or would, for lasting peace,
Ever be accounted for.
Nothing, now, can be done till spring.

Whether we shall have any crops to cut next year,
Today, remains unknown.
Six men from this parish never came back
To plant or harvest corn.
And the seeds, now lying in the barn unsown,
Remind me of the families of their children's children,
Who would have filled this church,
Had they been born.

November 11th 2008

Winter

Partridges

When walking in the countryside on these early winter days, more can often be seen, if clear weather allows, than perhaps might be expected at this time of year. Horizons are usually extended now that the trees are nearly naked, and the sun's lower angle in the sky shows up features in sharper relief, causing the folds and undulations of the valleys and hills to seem more pronounced. Familiar patterns, like the deeply fissured bark of old trees, or the style and character of stone walls, are emphasised in the sunlight of winter. With leaves almost gone and no tall grass or crops to provide cover, many of nature's secrets are now revealed. Hedges and trees no longer hide the nests of last season, now abandoned and filled with dead leaves, and hares, pheasants and foxes are much more in evidence in the relatively bare fields.

Just lately I've been keeping an eye on a covey of partridges. I first noticed the breeding pair on the margin of a wheat field in late spring, when young leverets could still be seen running amongst the drill rows. The first time I inadvertently disturbed them they burst into a short, whirring flight before gliding over the nearby hedge and disappearing. But every time I went near that place in the field afterwards, the pair were back in the same spot as before, and every time they were flushed again it was as though they had gone for good. Their wing beats are so fast that every few seconds they have to take a break and glide for fifty metres or so. They would sail over the hedge and disappear into the middle distance, melting into the growing crop beyond. After a while, it seemed as though they had bonded to the wheat field, secretly returning by some indirect route to their favourite spot after each rapid departure. They always stayed just far enough away from the hedge to be able to spot any potential predator, so they could spring into the air at a second's notice.

The partridges eventually nested on the far side of the field, taking plenty of time to choose the right place. A family of finches had already fledged and the cow parsley was high on the ditch banks before the eggs had been laid. The nest was no more than a shallow depression in the ground, lined with a few stems of dry grass and some dead leaves from the previous autumn. The hen partridge sat tight after laying the first egg, well screened by the fast growing wheat, while the cock bird stood guard and gathered food. As the hen nested she blended perfectly with the surrounding shades of browns and fawns of the limestone soil and fragments of last year's stubble. If she left the nest at all, she left no scent; the plundering badger or stoat passed by the beige and olive coloured eggs unaware, and thankfully, the marauding magpie did not see them.

As soon as the eggs hatched, nine chicks left the nest. They were born with the instinct of survival; if danger threatened, the little covey would spread out immediately and each chick, a tiny replica of its parents, would crouch motionless in the base of the grass on the field margin or in the cover of the corn. The hen was never far away, but she might rise in short flight and land again to lure a potential attacker away from her brood – she was ready to give up her life for them if necessary. She taught her chicks to hunt for insects amongst the undergrowth, and to sense approaching danger. After a few weeks, the covey could be seen making short flights above the corn, just as expertly as their parents. Before the summer ended three chicks vanished, probably falling prey to a sparrow-hawk or kestrel. Eventually the combine removed their cover of wheat, and they retreated to the field margins. The family is still together today, but as the eight birds take flight, it is now impossible to tell the chicks and adults apart; they are a lovely example of one of nature's most endearing family groups.

November 2007

The Coming of the Wolf Month

For a farmer, waking up in the morning to the sound of heavy rain falling is often the cause of some anxiety. There are usually some outstanding jobs on the 'to do' list which, because of wet conditions, will have to be postponed. But on the last day of October I listened to the falling rain, which marked the end of a wonderfully open spell of autumn weather, with a light heart and a fair degree of self-satisfaction. All the important outside jobs had been completed. For several weeks the farm tracks had been dry and firm enough to allow machinery easy access to distant fields, and we had just finished constructing two new culverts, which involved transporting and laying several huge concrete pipes. Thankfully, this job had been managed without marking the land or causing any damage. At the same time, some ditching work was carried out, along with the clearance of a fractured and sprawling willow tree of considerable age and size. One clear day, the air was spiced with the aroma of wood smoke as boughs of willow were cut and loaded on to a hissing, popping bonfire. The winter wheat had all been drilled a couple of weeks earlier, into ideal seedbeds. Germination was quick and young shoots were already emerging, slowly turning the fields from brown to green again as they relished a much needed drink. We had even managed to plough or cultivate all the blocks of land intended for planting next spring, well before winter set in.

These empty fields are almost deserted now; the joyful skylarks and exuberant swallows of just a few weeks ago have been replaced by idle crows and indignant rooks. They strut around belligerently over the bare land, occasionally taking flight to mob a passing buzzard or heron, shattering the peace with their raucous cries. With hardly a frost and little wind to speak of right up to the middle of November, autumn leaves stayed fixed on the trees for some time; the flame-coloured maples in the spinney by the lane shone out like beacons for ten days or so. Now, rotting leaves are thick on the ground underneath, and everything appears to be dead. But decay provides fertility, which in time will promote new growth; this is where primroses and cowslips will grow next spring. Sometimes, trees can change colour again in mid winter, long after leaves have fallen. Last Christmas I remember walking by the stream on a bright sunny morning, when a bitter east wind was blowing. I approached a large multi-stemmed alder growing out of the bank, and was struck by its colour, which seemed to have changed in a week. On that day it had an overall appearance of light burgundy, contrasting with the deep blue of the sky. From a short distance away the impression was that of a tree in blossom, but in fact the branches were bearing a myriad of newly emerged pink catkins. The searching wind continued to whistle thinly through the nearby bushes of bramble and thorn, singing its songs of winter, warning us of what was to come in the Wolf Month. This is the old Saxon name for January; starving wolves howled through the freezing midwinter nights of ages past, as the fear of wild beasts and the intense cold drew people closer together around their wood fires.

The natural sounds we hear today have been endlessly repeated for thousands of years; they are the unchanging sounds of the past, the present and the future. The atmospheric night time calls of wild animals, which must have been familiar to our ancestors, stir feelings of mystery in us all. The screeching of a vixen during the mating season and the eerie calls of tawny owls on starry frost-rimmed nights are haunting. The crackling of fire, rolling thunder or the sounds of water, whether flowing in a brook or swollen river, or gently lapping on the shores of a lake; the crashing of ocean waves, breaking with such power on the rocks, or rain softly falling; these are all evocations of memories past, buried deep within the human psyche. But for me it is the ever changing wind that creates the most primeval sound of all.

December 2009

Windsong

Do you remember how the wind, when in a certain quarter,
Outside our house would murmur and moan?
We have known many nights
When teasing ancient bricks and slates
And streaming past old walls of stone
The wind enchanted us, with mysterious music
In a wailing, melancholy tone;
The haunting sound rising and falling,
Like the baying of a distant hound,
Or a lonely owl, endlessly calling.

Do you remember when our little girl
Would take her flute and play?
Every crotchet and quaver
Piped with joy for us to savour,
Drawn into a melody
As sweet as breeze-blown flowers might be
In meadows, where they dance.

One day, we took a chance:
Sold up and moved away.
The new owners have added an extension
To the old house now,
But the wind, somehow, has lost its charm.
On stormy nights it tears at modern roof tiles,
And gusts at new-cut blocks of stone.
But the sound is not the same as it was before,
And our little girl's grown up and gone away;
The old music is no more.

Reflection, and a Storm

Now is a quiet period on the land, and there is time enough for reflection. I walk the fields on a dull mid winter day, contemplating the changes there have been over recent months. Summer had already grown old the day we cut the oats from this hill; I remember with pleasure larks hanging high in the blue of the harvest sky, and swallows darting low over golden rows of straw. A few days later, they gathered on the wires. Wheat grows here now, the young plants dormant in these short, cold days. Further on I cross over land which was ploughed in late autumn, where on a windy October day finches and sparrows flew restlessly in small flocks, rising from the stubble like flurries of leaves in a stiff breeze. Hundreds of seagulls arrived in this field within half an hour of the plough, and greedily stripped earthworms from the freshly turned soil as fast as they could, jostling for position and never more than ten yards from the mouldboards. Rooks came next, looking for grubs and beetles.

The sterility and the rich brown colours of freshly ploughed land do not last long. Quite soon a hare will come back to find shelter from the wind between the furrows, and the return of voles and shrews will not go unnoticed by kestrels and owls. Tiny green weed seedlings of charlock, speedwell and chickweed start to emerge slowly, along with volunteer cereal plants and other weeds; nature's paintbrush is still at work, even at this seemingly dead time of year. In the weeks since these fields were ploughed, rain and frost have started to crumble the thick slabs of clay into the beginnings of a seedbed; I plan to sow beans on this land in March, but winter is long in the fields, and even now is only about half way through.

Sometimes I refer to my diary to check what weather we had twelve months earlier, and I see that January 18th last year was very stormy. The wind had been gathering pace since early morning and as the sky darkened the gusts seemed to merge into one continuous blast, accompanied by a menacing roar. By mid morning there were creaking and rattling noises coming from all parts of the house, and just when we hoped the storm might be past its peak, the howl of the wind became even louder, and I half expected the chimneys to blow over and come plunging down to join us in the kitchen below. It was as though we were being besieged by a dreadful army, trying to break down the doors and force its way into the house. Above the roar of the wind we heard a sudden crash outside: several ridge tiles and a dozen slates had been ripped from the roof of the adjoining barn, landing in the courtyard where normally one or two cars would have been parked, but luckily the space was unoccupied on this day.

The first sheets of rain hit around lunchtime, blowing almost horizontally and sounding like gravel being hurled at the windows. The gale raged all afternoon, and just as darkness fell the lights went out. A telephone call informed us that a power line had been damaged by a falling tree. As the storm abated, we fumbled around in the gloom for candles and lanterns; before long the kitchen was lit by a cosy glow. We were glad of the Aga – at least we could still cook. At that point some friends arrived unexpectedly, and a very pleasant evening followed, catching up on everyone's news. We ate supper on our knees by a cheerful log fire, our faces glowing in the light from the flickering flames. When the power was eventually restored we all cheered spontaneously, but at that moment I almost resented electricity: the magic of candlelight was gone in a flash.

January 2008

Frozen Land - and Peewits

For those farmers who had outstanding ploughing and cultivation work to complete following the very wet autumn, the deep frosts of early January were a godsend. Frozen soil is similar in consistency to dry soil, and provided the frost is not too deep, it can be worked during hard weather, even though the ground may still have a high water content. A spell of good old-fashioned winter weather was just what was needed to allow us to catch up with land work, and my fields were frozen enough to take the weight of a tractor and implement for a few days at least, but not so frozen as to prevent penetration of the plough or subsoiler altogether. Mother Nature will now go to work over the coming weeks, breaking down the freshly cultivated land by degrees, with frost and sun, rain and wind, and the passing of time itself, all of which will slowly transform the clay soil into a friable tilth, suitable for planting beans in the spring.

On my first day out with the tractor and cultivator the bitterly cold conditions had created a clear, empty sky. Empty that is, for the first few minutes – a large flock of about a thousand hungry seagulls soon appeared seemingly from nowhere, hell bent on searching the freshly disturbed soil for anything that could be eaten. They followed the tractor up and down the field for hours. Eventually, they were joined by a few rooks, but the rooks always kept a short distance away from the gulls, only mixing with them briefly each time a fresh bout across the field was begun. After a while I was surprised to see a single peewit flying amongst the seagulls. Peewits (or lapwings) pair up well in advance of the breeding season, and just as I was thinking that its mate would not be far away, sure enough another peewit appeared. This was quite exciting: I hadn't seen these lovely birds on the farm for several months, and had accepted that, as they are on the RSPB's Red list, they must be in serious decline.

The following day I made an early start at 4am: I wanted to make the most of the opportunity provided by the frost. The first three hours were fairly uneventful, quite boring in fact; not much to see in the work lights apart from acres of frosted stubble passing by, but the John Deere has a good heater and an excellent CD player. Eventually the eastern horizon lightened and the sun came up after an interesting prelude of pink and violet wisps in the sky. A little later the rooks and seagulls returned, along with three pairs of peewits, and by mid morning about thirty peewits had formed into a little flock of their own. The seagulls of course always had the first chance of any worms or insects that might have been exposed from under the frozen crust, their clumsy flapping and bullying behaviour made sure of that; blundering tactics and sheer weight of numbers were no match for rook or peewit. The body language of the peewits was distinctly demure by comparison, patiently waiting their turn, and feeding much more selectively. Once they had settled on the ground, it was difficult to see them, their dark olive green bodies camouflaged against the soil. They would stay motionless until the tractor was almost upon them, only taking flight at the last second, suddenly visible as opening wings revealed white tips and a snowy white patch above the tail. It was as though, one by one, the peewits were actually rising from out of the ground itself. Once in flight their aerobatics are impressive. Rounded wings allow them to make impossibly tight turns and steep dives, and slow wing beats follow a graceful pattern; they never fly in straight lines.

By the third day the peewit flock had grown to about seventy birds. It was a relief to see them back on the farm again in such numbers; I hope that some of them stay and breed here as they did a few years ago. They are among the most attractive of farmland birds, with their dainty crests, artistic flight habit and plaintive cries. They nest out in the open on bare soil – a field of beans is ideal, there is plenty of space between the plants, and the growing beans provide just enough cover at the right time for the young brood. You hardly ever see a nest because they are so well camouflaged, but sometimes, in the vicinity, an adult bird will rise and fall in a peculiar wheeling motion as though injured. This clever imitation of impaired flight is designed to lead any potential predator away from the nest, by feigning a broken wing, and therefore the chance of easy prey. Tractor drivers probably enjoy as good a view of wildlife at close quarters as anyone without binoculars, and for a few more days the Arctic weather had its compensations as I enjoyed a vista of winter in the fields from the elevated position of my cab.

January 2009

Twilight Moods

I saw a skein of Canada geese the other day, flying gracefully across the winter sky. As is often the case, I heard the distinctive honking before the geese came into view. There were eleven birds (I am always compelled to count them for some reason) flying in a typical 'V' pattern, but sometimes wild geese also fly in a diagonal line. In either case the birds benefit from using less energy when flying in formation because of the slipstream created by the bird in front. No goose occupies the more demanding position of leader for long; each one takes its turn by rotation. Many birds are more noticeable in winter, particularly those living in hedges and gardens; the leaves which provide cover at other seasons are largely absent now. A glass door in our office opens out onto the garden, but we have not used it for a while, and an old cotoneaster close by has become overgrown with brambles, which have spread into the doorway. We have intentionally allowed this tangle of growth to remain, because it is such a pleasure to watch the antics of wrens through the glass, sometimes only a few inches away, busily hopping and darting about in the branches, constantly examining their surroundings and looking for insects and spiders. It's like having a window on the secret world of the wren.

Winter is only about halfway through, but increasing day length is a welcome sign of progress towards spring. The light lasts longer every day as twilight comes a little later each evening, fading into dusk before completing the transformation from day to night. The length of the twilight period is related to our distance from the equator; those living closer to it have less time to watch the sun go down. Everyone likes to watch beautiful sunsets; artists try to reproduce them, photographers try to capture them. As you gaze at the splendour, you feel that, should you turn away even for a few seconds, the spell will be broken and everything will have changed. Colourful skies can appear as the sun goes down at any time of the year, but a flaming sunset in the clear sharp air of winter is spectacular. Seeing the fiery red, pink and gold colours constantly changing as low-angle light bounces off particles of dust, ice crystals and smoke suspended in the air, is like watching a movie. Molecules of water vapour redden the light still further, as the rays of the sinking sun are reflected back and forth between clouds and the surface of the Earth, producing a painted sky.

I enjoyed a vivid winter sunset the other night as I headed home across the fields on the quad bike, after a couple of hours spent cutting up a fallen tree with the chainsaw. The visual treat was accompanied by the raucous cackle of pheasants flying home to their roosts and the smell of wood smoke as I approached the farmhouse. These are familiar sights, sounds and scents of winter. Sunset slowly gave way to twilight, and that soft velvety time when no matter what stresses and cares have prevailed during the day, a more tranquil mood takes over and you begin to unwind a little as dusk approaches. In the year 2000 we visited the Millennium Dome, which did not impress me much, except for the Rest Zone, which I liked. I'm sure the designers must have been inspired by their experiences of natural twilight and dusk, because in order to calm visitors, they had filled the curved, organic space with subdued lighting, constantly changing from one soft pastel shade to another, of such low intensity that a kind of artificial twilight was produced. The effect was enhanced by subtle aromas and gentle, soothing music, playing at low volume. It was a good attempt at reproducing the natural changes which occur at the end of each day, when primeval instincts are triggered in us all, along with the birds and animals. It signals the onset of a peaceful period of time when rest should be taken. Anything left undone now can wait until tomorrow.

January 2007

115

Ivy Round the Gate

Evergreen plants provide perhaps their most valuable contribution to the countryside during the winter months, when all else is leafless. Ivy is one of the few indigenous evergreens present amongst the trees and hedgerows of farmland, and its value to wildlife and landscape is often overlooked. The flowers appear from early autumn, and provide one of the last chances of the year for bees to collect late supplies of pollen and nectar. Ivy blossom attracts insects and end-of-season butterflies such as the comma, and the black fruits provide valuable food for birds in early spring. Ivy in moderation on some large trees is quite acceptable, but an excessive amount increases wind resistance and causes weakness, often contributing to the early demise of older trees. Once a tree becomes completely smothered it struggles to produce new growth and tends to 'give up'. Ivy is not a true parasite however, it only uses its host for mechanical support; it feeds from the soil via its own roots, relying on adhesive sucker like pads at the growing tips to secure itself to a tree or wall. Its reputation as a killer of trees, therefore, is not always deserved. A few months ago I decided to reduce the ivy growing on some of our larger trees on the farm. I don't want to be rid of it completely, but some control is necessary. Pulling ivy away from trees is not good for creatures which live and feed amongst the leaves and stems. Far better to use a less disruptive approach. My method of control is simply to cut out a chunk of each main stem at or close to ground level, leaving the rest of the plant to die back slowly over a period of months, thus allowing the creatures time to adapt. The ivy we cut last summer is still providing some shelter, and will continue to do so until it eventually falls away.

During World War II a small engineering business, owned and run by Geoff Bird, was evacuated from London to a modest workshop in Water Stratford. Geoff was a very creative and talented man, and for several years he earned his living repairing machinery and vehicles for local farmers. He made many individual items such as trailers, buck rakes and hay racks, and fabricated field and farm gates from angle iron and steel tube, many of which survive to this day, easily identifiable by their distinctive bow loop design. I know of some existing locally; one or two have become concealed in local hedgerows, 'grown in' and entwined with ivy where the gateway has not been used for many years. A good example of his artistry and blacksmithing skills is self evident in the lovely wrought iron garden gate he made which still stands at Church Gate, the cottage opposite St Giles Church, where he once lived. He also made an attractive ornamental iron gate for my parents, and it hung at the bottom of their drive during the 1950s. Eventually my father changed his Morris 8 for a larger car, for which the gateway was too narrow. New gateposts were set wider apart and a pair of wooden gates replaced the wrought iron one, which then spent several decades languishing in the nettles. Last summer I repaired it and had it shot blasted; we re painted it and hung it in our garden.

As a small boy I remember standing at that gate and watching the world go by through its hoops and twisted bars. I recall the huge black coal fired steamroller rumbling by as a gang of men worked away re surfacing the road, and the regiments of uniformed soldiers from the Army Camp at Tingewick marching through the village whilst on military exercises. A couple of days after the gate had been re hung, I had yet to become accustomed to seeing it in its new position. I was walking home from the fields to the garden, head down and deep in thought. When I looked up, the sight of the old gate, once so familiar, momentarily took me by surprise. In that brief instant I remembered the smell of the tar and the sound of a hundred pairs of hobnail boots.

February 2006

Concealed and Revealed

After a snow storm one January night a few winters ago, we noticed something strange next morning. Whilst all else was covered in a blanket of white, a perfectly circular patch of concrete, about six feet in diameter, in the yard between our back door and an outhouse, remained completely bare. At the time, there seemed to be no explanation. In any case, the snow soon melted and we quickly forgot all about it. Several weeks later however, things became clear. We had decided to carry out some alterations to the house, which involved removing the old concrete surface covering our back yard. Having first used a pneumatic drill to break up the concrete, we fetched the digger to remove the loose material. We started using the bucket on the back actor to pull the broken rubble into a heap, prior to loading it into a trailer ready to cart away. Suddenly there was an almighty crash and a huge cloud of dust rose up from behind the digger. When the air had cleared we cautiously investigated. The heap of rubble had disappeared, and there was now a large hole in the ground. Torchlight revealed the beautifully built stone shaft of an old well, thirty-seven feet deep and completely dry, right to the bottom! No-one today had known of the well's existence; it must have been abandoned a very long time ago, after which the half rotten oak cover was carelessly concealed under a thin layer of concrete, and then forgotten. We were extremely lucky that nobody had fallen down the well, particularly the man who had been operating the pneumatic drill.

I have since rebuilt the top of the shaft – it would have been a pity, I think, to have filled in the well; it must have originally been built with much hard labour and long forgotten skill, so we have made a feature of it and installed a safety grill. There have been some quite wet periods of weather in the last few years, but at no time has there been any water in the well, even when water has lain in hollow places in the garden nearby. This is a mystery; at one time the well must have provided a reliable supply of water to the house and farm buildings – we found the old hand pump, all seized up, in the loft of an old stable close by. There are now some interesting fern-like plants growing out from between the stones in the upper parts of the shaft; the seeds had been dormant for decades before exposure to daylight triggered their growth. The air that had been trapped inside the hidden well must have been relatively warm, hence the circular patch where the snow didn't settle.

February 2005

Crime Pays

After an overnight shower, the morning sun breaks through thinning cloud to enhance the green of the nearby wheat field and light up the view of the freshened landscape beyond. I should be enjoying this pleasant late winter morning, but I am upset. I am standing in one of my field gateways, surrounded by several black plastic bags overflowing with beer cans, fast food cartons and other rubbish, all of which have been dumped here, in broad daylight, within the last hour. What kind of mentality possesses the people who do these things? Clearly they have nothing but contempt for the countryside. Sadly, this kind of thing happens regularly nowadays, and we have had far worse, such as the dumping of tyres, fridges, old cars and furniture. Fly tipping is only the tip of the rural crime iceberg. Less visible, but even more unpleasant, is theft, now more common in the countryside than ever before, partly because tighter security in towns and cities has driven criminals to target softer rural areas.

Crime should not pay, but people break the law because they know that they are highly likely to get away with it. Almost every farmer I know in this district has suffered from theft in the last couple of years, some more than once. We became victims ourselves last August when early one morning we discovered that our stables had been burgled. The door to the tack room had been forced and £8,000 worth of saddles, bridles and equipment, belonging to the girls who keep their horses here, were missing. Then I realised that all our other buildings had been broken into, padlocks smashed and doors damaged. My chainsaws, hedge trimmer and brush cutter were gone, but the quad bike, which the thieves would have seen, was still there. I suppose they will be back for that another night. The culprits were likely to have been an organised gang of travelling criminals who steal to order, moving up and down the motorways in the middle of the night. The tack probably ended up in Ireland. Our theft was reported at 7.30am that morning, but it wasn't until 3.30 pm that a policeman, a stranger to North Bucks, came to begin taking statements. He was called away, but promised to return the next day. Six months have passed and we are still waiting…

When I started farming, most larger villages had their own policeman. Westbury had one, so did Tingewick. Respected members of the communities in which they lived and worked, they were friendly, helpful and approachable, and everyone knew them. You were just as likely to see them in the pub or in church as on duty in a police car patrolling the parishes. Their presence was reassuring, and on the whole, was a deterrent to criminals. This was simple, effective policing, but like most things that were once successful in this country, it has now been abandoned. Rural areas have become neglected as the police re-structure to fewer, larger forces, and many crimes like ours are not properly investigated because the police simply do not have enough time. Officers are required to spend so much time dealing with paperwork that many of them remain inside the police station for a large proportion of their working day. The increase in crime has created a huge demand for surveillance and security services; just look at all the companies in business today involved in the manufacture, supply and installation of burglar alarms, CCTV and associated equipment – theirs must be one of the fastest growing industries in the country. Since our robbery I have spent well in excess of a thousand pounds on alarm systems, and for the foreseeable future, I will have the annual maintenance fees to find too. Senior police have been warning the government for years that they cannot do their jobs properly because of ever-increasing bureaucracy. The government says that there are more police officers in this country than ever before; this may be true, but far too many of them are desk bound. Meanwhile, the outlook remains bleak as theft from farms and rural businesses increases, and unfortunately, crime continues to pay.

February 2007

Winter Blues

Who killed Cock Robin? Probably not the sparrow, with his bow and arrow. I found the little body on the lawn, under a pear tree. The most likely culprit would have been another cock robin. Competition for females is keen now that the mating season is about to begin, and robins are well known for fiercely defending their breeding and feeding territories. Aggressive behaviour sometimes leads them to attack their own reflections in windows or car wing mirrors in the mistaken belief that another robin is present and therefore poses a threat. Fights between rivals often end in death; it is not unusual to find a dead robin in the garden. Fatalities will also have been caused by the very cold weather. Small birds are at a disadvantage because they have the largest surface area relative to body mass, and therefore heat loss is quicker. Wrens are especially vulnerable, but owls and other raptors suffer not so much from the cold but from hunger because snow, which changes everything, conceals their prey. For eighteen months or so we have been seeing a barn owl quartering the grassy bank below the grain store, but I have not noticed it lately.

I was wondering, on a frosty morning in early January, how much longer the large crop of little crab apples would stay on their tree down by the stream. But that was before the snow. The bright yellow fruits, not much bigger than conkers, seemed to have been unaffected by the frosts of December, and remained fresh and unblemished. I got my answer two days later: heavy snowfall deprived the birds of their normal supplies of food, and drove them into the trees and hedges; the crab tree was almost stripped within hours. Bleached and broken skeletons of hogweed and dried out remnants of teasels poked out above the snow. These plants grew tall and stately along the banks of the stream last summer, attracting the attention of butterflies and bees. Now hungry birds were revisiting the wreckage for any remaining seeds.

Sunlit fields of dazzling snow provide a vivid contrast to the more usual drab appearance of the countryside in winter. It is difficult to believe that the intense whiteness is caused by nothing more than light, bouncing back and forth within the tiny air spaces of billions of minuscule ice crystals. Snow had been covering my winter wheat for several days, but I was not worried. Crops under a blanket of snow are well protected from the cruel icy winds coming from the north and east, and a patch of wheat by a wood, which had been grazed hard by rabbits, was given at least a temporary respite. On one of the snow-free days between Christmas and New Year, a light dusting of sleet on the ground served to highlight the patterns in the fields made at sowing time. Rows of green corn on a white background showed up clearly, emphasising each line and contour of the path the drill made over the land, the pattern marked at regular intervals by the tramlines.

Tramlines are created by a mechanism on the drill which prevents seed delivery to one or two pairs of coulters at predetermined intervals; these coulters are situated immediately behind the tractor's wheels. Two parallel unsown strips are thus established across the field at regular intervals, creating tracks which remain in place for the life of the crop. These tracks are then followed by the tractor driver each time fertiliser or pesticide is applied. Tramlines are equally spaced in multiples of the sowing width of the drill, so that they exactly fit the working width of the farm's sprayer and fertiliser spreader, which in our case is 24 metres. Our drill is 6 metres wide, so the tramline mechanism operates on every fourth bout of the drill.

Many people would probably pick February, if given the choice, as the month they would prefer to be away from England. This month is often perceived to be the most depressing of all, especially in the countryside, where cold winds seem endless and dreary days of mud and ice somehow accumulate into a mass of intolerable dullness. Farmers know that February is the best time to inspect a farm as a prospective tenant or purchaser, for it is in this month, when the land is usually wet, mostly devoid of foliage and apparently bleak and lifeless, that it looks its worst. People's behaviour is influenced by seasonal conditions, and just now there is a tendency to submit to a kind of lethargy which only prevails at this time of year. The days are still short, and the dampness does nothing to lift the spirits. Even if we have a dry spell, it will almost certainly remain cold. After working outside in such weather, the best place to be in the evenings is by the fireside, with a good book.

February 2010

Snow!

Even the most hard-hearted could not fail to have had their spirits lifted by the recent snow. The weather caused many problems of course, but the profound change to the landscape was exciting. How wonderfully the bare trees and hedges were enhanced, dressed in their icy clothes, and what peace there was in the quiet, snow-covered fields. Early on the morning after the first snow storm, the silence and the brightness were magical, simply because it was all completely new then, and such conditions are so unusual these days. Everything soon became charged with gleaming sunlight, evoking memories of snowy winters of old, much more commonplace in the past. For those youngsters who have never before seen several inches of snow lying for ten days or so in England, this new experience must have been thrilling, and no doubt provided a good deal of fun. Difficulties caused by the weather, such as the disruption of travelling arrangements, were tempered by the good old community spirit which always prevails in times of adversity, when smiling people look out for each other.

For the first few hours the snow remained pure and unspoiled, apart from the delicate prints of bird's claws seen in the garden and under our bird table where robins and finches had left their marks. Out in the fields the arrow shaped prints made by pheasants and crows were easily found near hedges and streams. Most wild animals stayed put at first: the badger snug and warm deep in his sett, the fox laid up in his earth, his bushy tail curled closely round his muzzle, and the rabbits quite still, huddled up to each other in their burrows. But after a while, hunger forces creatures into the open, and their presence is revealed by tracks in the snow.

Wild creatures carry on their normal activities every night of course, but grass, crops or bare ground do not normally provide much evidence of their passing. Tracks in snow are interesting because they not only tell who has passed by, but also reveal much about the individual's habits. Rabbit tracks are perhaps the most easily identifiable. A rabbit puts its front paws down first, and then 'leap frogs' its back legs over the front, leaving all four prints in a group. Hare tracks are similar, though bigger, with longer spaces between sets of prints, because the leap of a hare is sometimes as much as eight or ten feet. After the snow had been lying for a few days we saw an increase in the number of rabbit tracks crossing each other, giving the impression that more rabbits were about than actually was the case. Deer prints are easy to identify because of their sharp little cloven hooves, and a straight line of single paw prints is the track of a fox: he places his back feet in the same print as that made by his front feet. The evidence of violent events which have taken place the previous night is revealed when tracks abruptly become deeper, more scrambled and untidy than normal with greater disturbance of snow. This is where the chase began; the kill occurred a little distance away where the snow was stirred up and discoloured.

Any plant that is brave enough to flower in the depths of winter, especially during the severe weather of recently, deserves respect. We have two bushes of early honeysuckle, Lonicera purpusii. Both have scented different parts of the garden with their creamy blossom, and of the Viburnams, the fragrans seems to have been blooming continuously since autumn while the evergreen tinus has borne flowers since January. Mahonia and winter jasmine are also both in flower, and the Garrya Eliptica is now draped with its wonderfully long catkins. Twigs of Forsythia were cut, placed in water and brought indoors a few weeks ago, and now the colourful golden yellow flowers are bringing a welcome foretaste of spring into the house.

February 2009

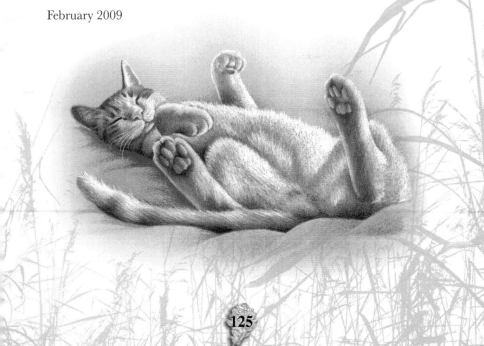

My Church

This is my church…
Anchoring the village at its lower end,
Halfway down the hill,
On the inside of a sharp, blind bend
Where traffic shares a moment with divinity.
Shaded in summer by canopies of leaf,
In winter framed by branches bare,
The grassy footpath underneath, though short,
Threads endlessly through hopeful lives
In search of an eternity.

Steadfast trees of hornbeam, chestnut, yew and lime,
Like sentinels of wisdom stand,
Half the age of time, or older.
I came here in early days
Carried on my father's shoulder,
Arriving at a reference point
Which both our lives would span:
My first Harvest Festival - a childhood memory,
The kind which never can
Embellished nor diminished be.

Little ever changes here.
But for the seasons, an air of constancy prevails;
Renewal is at first foretold
When early in the year, beside the path,
A messenger lays down a cloak of gold.
Sunlight on stone, warm to the touch,
Never fails to reassure;
As fine a place as any, this,
To watch the spring unfold.

And later, as the weather warms,
Perhaps in May or June,
The door is sometimes left ajar
In circumstances opportune
For birds to join in Sunday worship.
A chaffinch in the hedge nearby,
To fledglings, a sweet lullaby performs,
And singing from her hawthorn perch,
A few feet from the open door,
A jenny wren backs hymns and psalms
And every bird that loves this church
Contributes to the overture.

Even in the height of summer,
Within these medieval walls
The air's as cold as stone.
But fellowship there is to share,
And warm by contrast, is the kindly welcome shown
To strangers, friends and neighbours
When they come inside to pray
On major Christian festivals
Or any ordinary Sunday.

Occasionally, there is a wedding to enjoy,
Or perhaps a Christening.
And at Michaelmas, to every child's delight,
The conkers fall, for thanksgiving.
With shorter day and longer night,
Advent's promise is fulfilled
When softened hearts of young and old
By Christmas candlelight are thrilled.

A pleasure, too,
At the coldest time of year,
To be taken unawares
By a glimpse of summer,
When butterflies appear, during prayers.
A few will hibernate in here
And with the heat turned up,
Tapestry wings of finest weave
Open out and come alive,
Delicate as dew-fall on summer's eve.

And on the mornings of the brightest winter days,
When early sunbeams, lower slung,
Shine through the eastern stained-glass window,
Blinding rays turn gold
The wall on which a plaque is hung.
Six names once more in glory stand,
Proudly honoured now.
Those trusting lads at fate's behest
Forsook the anvil, lathe and plough,
To give up all that they possessed
For England.

Much to our predecessors we owe,
They who loved this place,
For their stewardship of yesterday
Ensured today's solace.
Past generations filled the church, many times the sum
Of those who gather here today,
But still we come.
The quest for spiritual life survives
Between the pages in the scrapbooks of materialistic lives
We come again in gladness,
And occasionally, in sorrow;
Seeking sanctuary on melancholy days,
Remembering those we shall not see tomorrow.

From time to time, cherished lives pass by;
The dead are laid to rest in sacred places,
Redundant bodies shed like worn out coats.
But the owners of those faces
Do not in this place lie;
Headstones bearing poignant quotes
Are hopelessly inadequate, yet nonetheless suffice
To tell the dates the dear departed left this world;
They wait for us in Paradise.

All that ever happened here
Seems bound up in suspense,
As though some epic will be told
In unknown ages hence.
For more than seven centuries
The warmth of human presence
Has seeped into these old walls;
When I'm alone in here, a resonance enthrals
With those who came so long ago.

I walk the path twixt church and trees, imagining
Ancient voices on the breeze,
Footprints in the snow
Of people summoned by the chimes
Of three high bells, all silent now;
In other times they welcomed folk
Through the Norman door below.
But this time is ours:
The way this little church still draws men in
Is as perennial as the wild flowers
That grow beneath the graveyard trees in spring.

We belong here,
No less than the bells in the tower,
The old stained glass,
The butterflies, the birds, the trees;
No less than the stones in the wall,
The flowers, the grass.
And in this time of ours
We have watched each season pass,
Seen people come and go;
Some have returned in later years,
Coming back to reclaim their church,
Like the swallows of forgotten springs.

It is my destiny
To share these things
With those who came before,
And he who comes after me will know
That he has found something special here,
Something for which he need no longer search.
When he comes,
Let him stand at this old oaken door,
With birdsong in his ear,
And say, "This is my church."

Sara Hack

The wildlife illustrations printed in "Seasons under my Sky" have been reproduced from colour pastel paintings by local artist Sara Hack. Sara is a professional illustrator for the Open University science faculty, but loves wildlife drawing and painting. She works mainly in pastel producing beautiful life like paintings of a wide variety of animals and birds. If you, or a relative have a favourite pet that you would like painted you can contact Sara by email at andy_hack@tiscali.co.uk to discuss a commission.

This publication was designed and produced by Andy Hack.

Acknowledgements

I am grateful to the following people who have helped me with this book:
Mike and Sara Edwards, for proofreading and grammatical guidance,
Andy Hack, for technical input, design and production,
Sara Hack, for permission to use her lovely illustrations,
Stephen Price, for marketing,
And to my wife Fiona, for her typing skills and general forbearance.

Further copies of this book may be purchased from the author.
Email: fiona@huntsmill.com or write to Huntsmill Farm, Shalstone,
Buckingham. MK18 5ND